MARVEL CINEMATIC UNIVERSE
PHASE ONE

MARVEL
IRON MAN

MARVEL CINEMATIC UNIVERSE
PHASE ONE

MARVEL

IRON MAN

Adapted by ALEX IRVINE

IRON MAN
Based on the screenplay by
Mark Fergus & Hawk Ostby and Art Marcum & Matt Holloway
Produced by Avi Arad, Kevin Feige
Directed by Jon Favreau

IRON MAN 2
Based on the screenplay by Justin Theroux
Produced by Kevin Feige
Directed by Jon Favreau

LITTLE, BROWN AND COMPANY
New York   Boston

Little, Brown and Company

Hachette Book Group
1290 Avenue of the Americas, New York, NY 10104
Visit us at lb-kids.com

Little, Brown and Company is a division of Hachette Book Group, Inc. The Little, Brown name and logo are trademarks of Hachette Book Group, Inc.

The publisher is not responsible for websites (or their content) that are not owned by the publisher.

First Edition: November 2014

Library of Congress Cataloging-in-Publication Data

Irvine, Alexander (Alexander C.)
Phase one: Iron Man / adapted by Alex Irvine.—First edition.
   pages cm.—(Marvel cinematic universe)
   ISBN 978-0-316-25634-6 (hardcover)
   1. Graphic novels. I. Iron Man (Motion picture) II. Title.
   PZ7.I673Phi 2014
   741.5'973—dc23
                                                          2014027636

10 9 8 7 6 5 4 3 2

RRD-H

Printed in the United States of America

CHAPTER 1

In a packed auditorium, Lieutenant Colonel James Rhodes, Tony Stark's best friend, stood at the podium and narrated as a film about Tony's life played on a huge screen behind him.

"Tony Stark. Visionary. Genius. American patriot. Even from an early age, the son of legendary weapons developer Howard Stark quickly steals the spotlight with his brilliant and unique mind.

"At age four, he builds his first circuit board.

"At age six, his first engine.

"And at seventeen, he graduates summa cum laude from MIT."

A picture of a smiling young Tony dissolved into a portrait of his father, Howard. Rhodey went on, his tone somber. "Then, the passing of a titan. Howard Stark's lifelong friend and ally, Obadiah Stane, steps in to help fill the gap left by the legendary founder, until, at age twenty-one, the prodigal son returns and is anointed the new CEO of Stark Industries."

Another series of pictures showed Tony's incredible successes at Stark Industries. "With the keys to the kingdom," Rhodey went on, "Tony ushers in a new era for his father's legacy, creating smarter weapons, advanced robotics, satellite targeting. Today, Tony Stark has changed the face of the weapons industry by ensuring freedom and protecting America and her interests around the globe."

Rhodey paused as the slide show ended. "As liaison to Stark Industries," he said, "I've had the unique privilege of serving with a real patriot. He is my friend and he is my great mentor. Ladies and gentlemen," Rhodey finished, pointing off to one side, "this year's Apogee Award winner...Mr. Tony Stark."

The crowd broke into thunderous applause. A spotlight moved across the stage and landed on...an empty chair. The applause quickly faded into surprised mur-murings.

Rhodey gritted his teeth as Obadiah Stane, Stark Industries's second-in-command, strode out onto the stage and took the podium. The spotlight shone on his shaven head.

"Thank you, Colonel," he said, accepting the award statuette.

"Thanks for the save," Rhodey said, away from the microphone so the crowd wouldn't hear.

Stane nodded and stepped to the podium. "This is beautiful. Thank you," he said. "Thank you all very much. This is wonderful."

He looked at the statuette for a long moment and then said, "Well, I'm not Tony Stark. But if I were, I'd tell you how honored I am and…what a joy it is to receive this award." He took a deep breath and forced a grin. "The best thing about Tony is also the worst thing—he's always working."

Tony was not working. Rhodey found that out right away. In a nearby casino, Tony sat at a gaming table, betting enormous amounts of money. He paused and threw the dice, turning up another winner. The crowd around the table cheered.

Tony spotted Rhodey across the casino floor striding toward him. "You are unbelievable," Rhodey said when he reached the table.

"Oh no!" Tony exclaimed. "Did they rope you into this awards thing?"

Rhodey scowled at him. "Nobody roped me into anything. But they said you'd be deeply honored if I presented the award."

"Of course I'd be deeply honored," Tony said. "And it's you. That's great. So when do we do it?"

Rhodey plopped the Apogee Award down on the gaming table. "Here you go."

Tony stared at it, surprised. "There it is," he said. "That was easy." When he saw that Rhodey was still irritated, he got a little more serious. "I'm so sorry."

Rhodey waved the apology away. "Yeah, it's okay."

Tony held up his dice to one of the women next to him at the table. "Give me a hand, will you?" he asked. "Give me a little something-something."

She smiled and blew on the dice for good luck.

Tony held the dice out to Rhodey then. "Okay, you too."

"I don't blow on dice," Rhodey said.

But Tony talked him into making the roll instead. He picked up the dice, shook them, and rolled—but they came up losers. The crowd around the table sighed and glared at Rhodey. Tony didn't seem bothered, though. He collected a huge stack of chips from the table and headed for the door with Rhodey. People gawked and took pictures of him with their cell phones.

"A lot of people would kill to have their name on that award," Rhodey said angrily. "What's wrong with you?"

"Hold that thought," Tony said, and strode toward the restroom. Once inside, he splashed water on his face.

"A thousand people came here tonight to honor you, and you didn't even show up," Rhodey said, following him. "Now you're going into a war zone tomorrow just for an equipment demo. We should be doing that here in Nevada."

Tony sighed. "This system has to be demonstrated under true field conditions."

Just then, the door to the restroom swung open and a woman in her late twenties walked in. Rhodey recognized Virginia "Pepper" Potts, Tony's executive assistant. She wasn't the kind of person who let a MEN'S ROOM sign get in the way of doing her job.

"Tony, you're leaving the country for a week," she said,

following him as he dropped the Apogee Award in the tip basket and went back onto the casino floor. "I just need five minutes of your time."

Before Tony could answer, a young woman holding a digital voice recorder pushed her way through the crowd. "Mr. Stark!" she called. "Christine Everhart, journalist. Can I ask you a few questions?"

"Can I ask you a few back?" Tony replied, slowing down to talk.

"You've been described as the da Vinci of our times," Ms. Everhart said. "What do you say to that?"

"Ridiculous," Tony said. "I don't paint."

"And what do you have to say about your other nickname: the Merchant of Death?"

Tony shrugged. "That's not bad." He sized her up, figuring from her appearance and accent that she was one of those do-gooder journalists who came from a privileged background and had never spent a day in the real world. "Let me guess," he said. "Berkeley?"

"Brown, actually," she said.

"Well," he said, "it's an imperfect world, but it's the only one we've got. The day that weapons are no longer needed to keep the peace, I'll start manufacturing bricks and beams to make hospitals."

"Rehearse that much, Mr. Stark?" Ms. Everhart asked.

"Every night in front of the mirror. But call me Tony."

She frowned. "All I want is a serious answer."

"Okay, here's serious," he said. "My old man had a philosophy: Peace means having a bigger stick than the other guy."

"That's a great line, coming from the guy selling the sticks," she shot back.

Now Tony was starting to lose his patience. "My father helped defeat the Nazis. He worked on the Manhattan Project. A lot of people, including your professors at Brown, would call that being a hero."

She didn't bat an eyelash. "And a lot of people would also call that war profiteering."

"When do you plan to report on the millions of people we've saved by advancing medical technology? Or the millions more we've kept from starving with our intelli-crops? All those breakthroughs came from military funding, honey."

"Did you ever lose an hour of sleep in your whole life?" she asked him. Now her temper was up, too.

Tony winked at her. It was time to defuse the situation.

CHAPTER 2

Tony Stark's home was a sprawling, ultramodern mansion atop a tall bluff on the edge of the Pacific Ocean, with a commanding view of the surf far below. Tony wasn't admiring the view, though. As usual, he was working in the huge laboratory-garage beneath the mansion. This morning, his project was tuning up one of the cars in his collection, an old '32 Ford. He looked up as Pepper entered the workshop.

"Boss," she said, "you still owe me five minutes—"

"Just five?" he asked, cutting in. "We really should

spend more quality time together." He smiled at her, but she merely sighed.

"Focus," she said. "I need to leave on time today."

"Why the rush?" he asked. Tony gazed into her eyes. "You have plans tonight, don't you?"

Pepper lifted her perfect nose just slightly. "I'm allowed to have plans on my birthday."

"It's your birthday again?" Tony said.

"Yep," she replied. "Funny—same day as last year."

"Well, get yourself something nice from me," he said.

"I already did," Pepper said, smiling indulgently. "Thank you, Mr. Stark."

"You're welcome, Ms. Potts."

James Rhodes paced the tarmac. "Where is he?" he grumbled. Behind him, Tony's private jet sat waiting.

Just then, a sports car roared up, a limousine right beside it. Tony's chauffeur, Happy Hogan, popped open the trunk and pulled out Tony's overnight suitcase. Tony hopped out of the car and headed directly toward the jet. "You're good," he said to Happy. "Thought I lost you back there."

"You did," Happy said. "I had to cut across Mulholland."

Rhodey followed Tony to the plane, fuming. "I was standing out there for three hours!"

Tony stopped at the top of the stairs to his plane, a custom-built jet bearing the company slogan: STARK INDUSTRIES—TOMORROW TODAY. "Waiting on you now," he said. "Let's go. Wheels up! Rock and roll!"

Shaking his head, Rhodey followed Tony.

The flight attendant shut the cabin door as Tony and Rhodey settled into the jet's plush leather seats.

After dinner, Rhodey and Tony got into another argument. "You just don't get it," Rhodey said, annoyed. "I don't work for the military because they paid for my education; it's a responsibility to our country."

Tony regarded his friend coolly. "All I said was, with your smarts and your engineering background, you could write your own ticket in the private sector." He flashed a smile. "And working as a civilian," Tony continued, "you wouldn't have to wear that military straitjacket."

"Straitjacket?" Now Rhodey wasn't just annoyed. He was angry. He unbuckled himself and got up to move away from Tony. "You know, the heck with you," Rhodey said. "I'm not talking to you anymore."

One of the flight attendants brought a tray with a bottle and two glasses.

"We're working right now," Rhodey insisted.

But after a while, he wasn't as angry anymore. Tony was Tony; what could you do?

The next morning, they touched down in Bagram Air Force Base in Afghanistan. Once there, a convoy of Humvees took them from the base to a fortified test site in the desert. As Rhodey settled in among the generals and VIPs, Tony went to work. He walked up and down the makeshift stage, boasting the virtues of Stark Industries's latest equipment.

"The age-old question," Tony said, "is whether it's better to be feared or respected. I say, is it too much to ask for both?"

His eyes gleamed as he walked over to a Jericho missile perched atop a mobile launcher.

"With that in mind," Tony continued, "I present the

crown jewel of Stark Industries's Freedom Line of armaments. This is the first missile to incorporate my proprietary Repulsor Technology—or RT, as we like to call it. A breakthrough in energy control and guidance."

He pressed a button on a remote, and the missile streaked into the air. The rocket arced gracefully toward a nearby rocky mountain peak.

"Fire off one of these babies," Tony said, "and I guarantee the enemy is not going to leave their caves. For your consideration...the power of Jericho."

He pointed as the Jericho missile divided from a single weapon into a swarm of minimissiles. The missiles smashed into the nearby peak. With a deafening roar, the mountain exploded into a shower of debris.

Dust washed over Tony and the generals. Tony continued smiling, unfazed by the sudden blast. When the smoke cleared, much of the mountaintop was gone. The generals and Afghan officials nodded and muttered among themselves, impressed.

"Gentlemen," Tony said, "Stark Industries operators are standing by to take your orders." He walked off the stage to where Rhodey stood waiting.

"I think that went well," Tony whispered to his friend.

Rhodey started to say something, but Tony was already answering his satellite videophone. He punched a button and Obadiah Stane's weary face appeared on the screen.

"Obie, what are you doing up so late?" Tony asked.

"I couldn't sleep until I found out how it went," Stane replied. "How did it go?"

Stark grinned. "I think we've got an early Christmas coming."

"Way to go, my boy," Stane replied blearily.

"Why aren't you wearing those pajamas I got you?" Tony asked.

"Good night, Tony," Stane said, and hung up.

Tony passed the phone to Rhodey, and then walked over to a row of soldiers waiting by the group's Humvees. "All right," Tony said, "who wants to ride with me?" Reading the name tag of a young soldier nearby, he asked, "Jimmy?"

Jimmy's young face lit up. "Me?" The two soldiers with him—Ramirez and Pratt, according to their name tags—nodded as well. Tony and the three soldiers piled into the vehicle. Rhodey was about to get in as well, but Tony stopped him.

"I'm sorry," he said. "This is the Fun-Vee. The Hum-Drum-Vee is back there."

The look he got from Rhodey was part bemusement and part irritation. "Nice job," Rhodey said.

Tony accepted the compliment like he deserved it. "See you back at base," he said.

As Rhodey headed for another vehicle, Tony slammed the door shut. Ramirez cranked up the stereo, and their Humvee roared off into the desert.

CHAPTER 3

Tony watched as the bleak landscape of Afghanistan rushed past the Humvee's window. The vehicle was cramped, sweaty, and hot—a far cry from the air-conditioned luxury Tony had known all his life. He adjusted the collar of his expensive suit and glanced at the soldiers riding with him. None of them seemed bothered by the heat or the bumpy road. Buried under their gear, all three soldiers looked alike to Tony.

"Oh, I get it," Tony said after a time. "You guys aren't allowed to talk. Is that it?"

"No," Jimmy replied. "We're allowed to talk."

Ramirez flashed Tony a smile. "I think these boys are just intimidated."

Tony nearly jumped. "You're a woman!" he blurted.

The other soldiers chuckled.

Tony's face reddened as he straightened up in his seat. "I would apologize for not realizing, but isn't that what we're fighting here for? The right of all people to be equal?" He smiled back at her, but Ramirez merely shook her head.

"Mr. Stark, sir?" Pratt asked. "Is it cool if I take a picture with you?"

"Yes. It's very cool," Tony said. Then he added, "I don't want to see this on your page."

Grinning, Pratt crowded next to Tony as Jimmy framed them in a digital camera. Tony unbuckled his seat belt and put his arm around Pratt's shoulder. One of them was making a peace sign.

Just then, a huge explosion rocked the truck. Tony watched through the windshield as an enormous ball of fire knocked the Humvee ahead of them off the dirt road.

Tony slammed into the side of the Humvee. His gaze fell on the right side-view mirror just as the Humvee behind them blew up.

Trapped between two burning vehicles, Tony's Humvee skidded to a stop. The sound of gunfire rattled the

Humvee's windows. *Rhodey was right,* Tony thought. *We should have done this in Nevada.*

"Stay here!" Pratt commanded. He, Ramirez, and Jimmy piled out of the Humvee, ready to fight. As they left, another explosion filled the air with dust.

Tony peered out the window, trying to see what was happening. The soldiers took up defensive positions, firing through the clouds of dust kicked up by the bomb. One of them ran into the billowing cloud, trying to secure the Humvee's position.

As Tony ducked down, yet another explosion rocked the vehicle, shattering the window above his head. A shower of glass rained down on Tony's two-hundred-dollar haircut. He knew he was doomed if he stayed in the Humvee. So he scrambled across the seat and out the far door.

Tony stumbled across the rugged landscape, looking for cover. Smoke stung his eyes and the sound of gunfire echoed in his head. The whole convoy had ground to a halt. They were trapped.

Something landed nearby with a soft thud—an unexploded rocket-propelled grenade. Tony gaped at the info stenciled on the side of the explosive: USM 11676—STARK MUNITIONS.

The enemy was shooting at him with weapons made

by his company. Tony turned and ran. *Please let it be a dud!* he thought. *Please let it be—*

A blaze of blinding white light surrounded him as the grenade went off. The blast hurled Tony through the air and he landed hard on the ground. The air rushed out of his lungs, and the world around him faded away.

When Tony came to, he found himself tied to a chair in a dark cave. Ragged, makeshift bandages covered his body. Every part of him hurt—especially his chest. It was all he could do to stay conscious.

Two scruffy guards, armed with machine guns, stood nearby. On the other side of the cave, a video camera focused on a tall man who seemed to be the leader of these people. Tony realized the men must be insurgents—the rebel fighters who had attacked his convoy. The tall man read a prepared statement for the camera in a language Tony didn't understand, probably Arabic or Pashto. Next to him stood a line of armed, hooded men holding up a banner showing ten interlocking rings—a sign Tony had seen before on the news. It was the symbol of a well-known insurgent faction.

The leader finished reading and thrust a huge knife into the air. The others cried their approval. The cameraman turned the camera toward Tony. The leader stepped forward, his knife gleaming in the semidarkness. Thankfully, Tony passed out.

When Tony opened his eyes again, he was in some kind of emergency room—though it didn't look like a very good one. He was strapped to a bed and connected to numerous wires and tubes. Everything around him, even the medical equipment, looked dirty and ill-repaired. An aging man in a dirty doctor's smock stood by a nearby sink, shaving. He didn't notice that Tony had woken up.

Feeling thirsty, Tony reached for a pitcher of water on a nearby table, but the tubes and wires connecting him to the medical machines wouldn't let him stretch that far. He grabbed hold of the wires and pulled, trying to rip them out. Somehow, he didn't have the strength. His chest ached terribly.

The doctor noticed his efforts. "I wouldn't do that if I were you," he said in slightly accented English. His dark eyes strayed meaningfully down the wires to a nearby car battery. A chill rushed down Tony's spine. Who were these people? What had they done to him?

He put his hand on his bandaged chest and remembered he was in the hands of the enemy. He'd been taken prisoner—and they'd done something to his heart.

CHAPTER 4

Tony faded in and out of consciousness for a long time. When he could finally focus again, he was in a cave. The doctor stood a dozen yards away, stirring a bubbling pot over a small gas-fired furnace. It looked like he was working on an experiment. Flickering fluorescent lights dangled overhead. A closed metal door seemed to be the room's sole exit. Dirt, grease, and blood stained the doctor's yellowed smock. He had a tanned, wrinkled face, gray hair, and thick glasses. He glanced over as Tony stirred.

Tony looked at his chest and gasped. Some kind of

bulky metal machine protruded from beneath his fresh bandages.

"What have you done to me?" he asked.

The doctor stopped stirring the pot. "My name is Yinsen, and what I did is to save your life. I removed all the shrapnel I could, but there's a lot left and it's headed into your atrial septum." He picked up a jar from a nearby shelf and tossed it to Tony. "Here, want to see? I have a souvenir."

Tony, who was no longer strapped down, caught the jar and winced. It was full of shrapnel. His chest felt very, very strange.

"What is this?" he asked, looking down at his chest.

"That is an electromagnet, hooked up to a car battery, and it's keeping the shrapnel from entering your heart." Tony looked at his wound and suddenly felt sick. He looked away from it at the nearby car battery. Then he noticed a security camera perched high on the cave wall.

Yinsen nodded. "That's right. Smile."

Somehow, Tony didn't feel like smiling.

"We've met once before," Yinsen continued, stirring the pot, "at a technical conference in Bern, Switzerland."

"I don't remember," Tony said.

"You wouldn't," Yinsen replied. "If I'd been that drunk, I wouldn't have been able to stand."

Tony brushed this off. "Where are we?" he asked. Before Yinsen could answer, a metal slat in the middle of the door slid back, revealing two menacing eyes.

Yinsen stopped stirring. "Stand up!" he hissed at Tony. "Do as I do. Now!"

Tony tried to stand, but couldn't manage it. Yinsen dropped his spoon and helped Tony up. Before Tony could ask what was happening, the door swung open and a tall, powerful-looking man entered, flanked by two armed henchmen.

The man began speaking in Arabic and Yinsen translated. "Abu Bakar says, 'Welcome, Tony Stark, the greatest mass murderer in the history of America. It is a great honor.'"

Abu Bakar held out a surveillance photo showing an image of the Jericho missile test. He continued talking.

"You will build for him the Jericho missile you were demonstrating," Yinsen translated.

Tony took a deep breath. His chest ached dully. "I... refuse," he said.

Yinsen leaped forward and slapped Tony across the face. Yinsen's eyes burned with anger. "You refuse?" he raged. "This is the great Abu Bakar! You are alive only because of his generosity. You are nothing. Nothing! He offers you his hospitality, and you answer with insolence? Obey him or you will die!"

Tony's cheek stung. He took a step back.

Abu Bakar chuckled. Then, with a nod of satisfaction to Yinsen, he turned and left. The guards went with him. As the door slammed behind them, Yinsen let out a sigh of relief.

"Perfect," he said. "You did very well, Stark. Good."

Tony sat back down on his cot, confused.

Yinsen smiled. "I think they're starting to trust me." He returned to his kettle. Tony realized suddenly that Yinsen wasn't working on an experiment—he was cooking.

Tony's stomach growled. "What's next?" he asked.

Yinsen shrugged. "We've reached the end of my plan," he said. "From now on, we improvise."

The next day, guards came for both of them and led them, hooded, through the cave passages. Tony walked blindly for long minutes until one of Abu Bakar's henchmen yanked the smelly hood off of his head. Blinking against the sudden light, Tony found himself in a valley surrounded by tall mountains. The day's brightness stung his eyes, and it took him a moment to process all he was seeing.

Skids piled with weapons surrounded him. All of the munitions—some dating back twenty years—bore the Stark Industries logo. Abu Bakar said something.

"He wants to know what you think," Yinsen said.

Tony shook his head in disbelief. "I think you got a lot of my weapons."

Abu Bakar spoke again.

"As you can see," Yinsen translated, "Abu Bakar has everything you will need to build the Jericho. He wants you to make a list of materials. He says for you to start working immediately."

Tony looked around the valley, his eyes settling on a man nearby. He recognized the man from military briefings; he was a warlord called Raza—a leader of the Ten Rings rebels.

"When you are done," Yinsen said, still translating, "he will set you free."

"No, he won't," Tony said, keeping up a smile for appearances.

"No," Yinsen agreed quietly. "He won't."

General Gabriel walked alongside Rhodey as he picked through the charred wreckage from the ambush. "What a mess," the general said, shaking his head.

"Something's not right," Rhodey said.

"It looks like a standard hit-and-run to me," the general replied.

"Sir, I'm telling you, this was a snatch-and-grab," Rhodey insisted. "As soon as they got what they wanted, they melted away—and what they wanted was Tony Stark."

"Intel's on it," Gabriel said. "If Stark is out there, we'll get him back."

Rhodey took a deep breath. "General, with your permission, I'd like to stay and head up the search."

"Negative," Gabriel replied. "Right now, the best way for you to serve your country is to get back to the United States and handle the firestorm of publicity."

"Tony Stark is the Department of Defense's number one intellectual asset," Rhodey countered. "I can be of more value in the field, getting him back."

"Duly noted," the general replied. "But we need you back home." He turned and walked toward his staff car.

"Lieutenant Colonel," he called back, "it is not lost on me that you and Stark are lifelong friends, but—in this instance—there's nothing I can do."

A few days later, Tony, wrapped in an army surplus blanket, sat next to Yinsen's portable furnace. Yinsen was cooking again. Tony wondered if he ever used the furnace for anything else.

"I'm sure your people are looking for you, Stark," Yinsen said, "but they will never find you in these mountains. What you just saw is your legacy—your life's work in the hands of these murderers."

Tony said nothing.

"Is that how you want to go out?" Yinsen asked. "Sitting silently in a cave? Is this the last act of defiance of the great Tony Stark? Or are you going to try to do something about it?"

Tony rubbed his head. "Why should I do anything?" he asked. "They're either going to kill me now, or the shrapnel will kill me in a week."

Yinsen looked into his eyes. "Then this is a very important week for you."

CHAPTER 5

A bu Bakar turned on the lab's new portable generator.

"Okay," Tony said, trying to think of a way out of the mess he'd gotten himself into, "here's what I need to build your weapons..."

Yinsen cleared his throat and began translating Tony's list for Abu Bakar.

"S-category missiles," Tony said. "Lot 7043. The S-30 explosive tritonal, and a dozen of the S-76. Mortars: M-Category, numbers one, four, eight, twenty, and sixty.

M-229s—I need eleven of these. Mines: the pre-nineties AP fours and AP sixteens."

Abu Bakar relayed the orders and his men hurried off to fill Tony's requests.

Tony made an arc with his hands. "I need this area free of clutter," he said, "with good light. I want the equipment at twelve o'clock to the door, to avoid logjams. I need welding gear—acetylene or propane—helmets, soldering setup with goggles, and smelting cups. Two full sets of precision tools..."

Abu Bakar seemed annoyed by the long list.

"Finally," Tony said, "I want three pairs of white tube socks, a toothbrush, protein powder, spices, sugar, five pounds of tea, playing cards, and...a washing machine and dryer."

Abu Bakar pushed his face right up to Tony's and spoke in Arabic.

"A washing machine?" Yinsen translated. "Do you think he's a fool?"

Tony stared into the insurgent's eyes. "I must have everything," he said. "Great man will make a big boom for the powerful Abu Bakar. Big boom will kill Abu Bakar's enemies."

Yinsen translated and, slowly, Abu Bakar nodded and smiled.

The next day, Tony and Yinsen began salvaging the pieces they needed from the aging weapons Abu Bakar's men had brought.

"You know that Abu Bakar removed all the explosives from these before he gave them to us," Yinsen whispered.

"I know," Tony replied. "They're crazy, not stupid." He carefully removed a tiny strip of palladium metal from one of the missiles. "Okay, we don't need this," he said, gesturing to the rest of the missile's guidance machinery.

"What is that?" Yinsen asked.

"That's palladium. Oh point one five grams. We need at least one point six, so why don't you break down the other eleven?"

When they were all together, Tony and Yinsen put the palladium strips in a melting bowl. "Good," Tony said. "Now heat the palladium to 1,825 degrees Kelvin." That was when the palladium would melt.

As Yinsen heated the metal, Tony wrapped a copper

coil around a glass ring he'd removed from another missile. They had a lot to do, and not much time.

"Careful…" Tony said as Yinsen brought him the melted palladium.

"Relax," Yinsen replied. "I have steady hands. It's why you're still alive."

They poured the palladium into the ring and waited until it cooled. Then Tony finished connecting the last pieces of the device and threw the lab generator switch. The lights in the cave dimmed and the palm-sized device glowed atop the workbench.

"That doesn't look like a Jericho missile," Yinsen observed.

"That's because it's a miniaturized Arc Reactor," Tony said. "I got a big one powering my factory at home. It should keep the shrapnel out of my heart." He had used a version of what he called Repulsor Technology to hold the shrapnel in place.

Yinsen nodded, understanding. "So you won't need the car battery anymore."

"Yeah," Tony said. "And this power source will last a bit longer than a week."

Yinsen leaned close, studying the device. "It's pretty small," he said. "What can it generate?"

"Three gigajoules, give or take."

Yinsen's mouth dropped open. "That could power your chest plate for fifty lifetimes!"

A sly grin crept over Tony's face. "Or something really big for fifteen minutes." He held Yinsen's eyes for a moment and then said, "Let's install it in my chest."

Yinsen glanced at the security monitor that was tucked into a corner of the cave ceiling. "They'll be watching."

"Then I'll be counting on those famously steady hands to work quickly...and in secret," Tony said.

Over the next few weeks, they fell into a routine. Work, sleep, dodge the newest threats from the insurgents. Repeat. The laboratory was strewn with parts that might, for all his captors knew, be assembled into a high-tech missile. After a long day spent cutting, welding, and shaping salvaged sheet metal, Tony looked over at Yinsen. He seemed to be assembling some kind of game.

"What are you doing?" Tony asked.

Yinsen looked up. "Tell me what you're doing, and I'll tell you what I'm doing."

"It looks like you're making a backgammon board."

"I'm impressed," Yinsen said. "How about we play, and if I win, you tell me what you're really making."

"Two things," Tony said. "One, I don't know what you're talking about. Two, I was the backgammon champ at MIT four years running."

"Interesting," Yinsen replied. "I was the champion at Cambridge—the one in England."

Tony leaned away from his work and rolled his eyes. "Please don't use the words 'interesting' and 'Cambridge' in the same sentence. Is Cambridge still a school?"

"It's a university. You probably haven't heard about it since Americans can't get in."

Tony shot him a look. "Unless they're teaching."

Just at that moment, the door to the lab flew open and Abu Bakar stormed in, followed by four of Raza's guards. The guards took up positions on either side of the room and pointed their guns at Tony and Yinsen. After the room was secure, Raza entered. Everything about him screamed "danger." He seemed unpredictable and deadly.

"Relax," Raza told Tony. He walked to the workbench and looked at the missile schematics Tony had drawn on salvaged pieces of paper.

"The bow and arrow was once the pinnacle of weapons

technology," Raza mused. "It allowed Genghis Khan to rule from the Pacific to the Ukraine."

The warlord fixed his cold eyes upon Tony. "Today, whoever has the latest Stark weapons rules these lands. Soon, it will be my turn." Seeming to sense something was amiss, he turned to Yinsen and spoke in Urdu.

Yinsen shook his head and replied, adding in English, "We're working. The missile is very complex. That's why we're taking so long. We're working very hard. Ask Stark if you don't believe me."

Raza glanced at Stark. Tony remained stoic.

At a nod from the warlord, the guards seized Yinsen and forced him to his knees. Raza stepped forward and brought a piece of red-hot metal from the furnace, holding it closer to Yinsen's face as he kept on asking questions in Urdu, or whatever language he spoke.

Tony started to panic. He needed Yinsen, and he couldn't just stand there and watch someone be tortured for protecting him. "What do you want?" he shouted at Raza. "A delivery date?"

He pointed at Yinsen. "I need him! Good assistant!"

Raza glared at him for a long moment. Then he flung the glowing metal rod away. The guards let go of Yinsen, and he collapsed to the floor.

Raza scowled at Yinsen and Tony. "You have until to-morrow to assemble my missile," he said. He turned and left the room. The others followed, locking the door as they left. Tony helped Yinsen to his feet.

Yinsen recovered for a few minutes and then said, "Now are you going to tell me what you're really building?"

Tony looked at Yinsen. Even after all they'd been through together, could he trust him? Tony decided he could. Being careful to avoid the gaze of the surveillance camera, he showed Yinsen the real plans for the project.

Yinsen's weathered face broke into a smile.

Their backgammon game would have to wait.

Over the following twenty-four hours, the two of them worked feverishly: soldering circuits, connecting electron-ics, hammering metal—always carefully concealing their purpose from the watchful eyes of the warlord and his guards.

"My people have a tale about a prince," Yinsen said as he worked the salvaged metal. "The king hated the prince, so he banished him to the underworld and jailed him there."

Sweat poured from Tony's body as he beat the metal into shape. "Tell me," he said.

"The king made the prince work the iron pits. Year after year, the prince mined the heavy ore, becoming so strong he could crush pieces of it together in his bare hands."

Tony wiped the soot from his face.

"Too late the king realized his mistake," Yinsen continued. "He took his finest sword and went to kill the prince. But when he struck, the sword broke in half. The prince himself had become as strong as iron."

Tony lifted a glowing iron mask from the furnace. The mask was crude, but it would definitely suit his purpose.

"What next, young prince?" Yinsen asked.

CHAPTER 6

Pepper strode down the executive hallway at Stark Industries headquarters, aimed straight for Rhodey and Obadiah Stane. They were engrossed in conversation. Both men looked upset, and Pepper knew why. She was upset, too. Not just upset. Furious.

As she approached, Stane sighed and went into his office. Rhodey headed for the door, but Pepper intercepted him.

"So that's it?" she asked angrily. "You're giving up the search for Tony? Everyone's pulling the plug and moving on?"

Rhodey shook his head. "There's nothing left we can do. It's been weeks. If there was any indication that Tony was still alive—"

"Spare me," Pepper interjected. "I read the official e-mail. I thought that maybe, as Tony's best friend, you'd have something different to say."

She turned on her heel and stormed into her office. Rhodey followed.

"Pepper—" he began. But before Rhodey could say another word, Pepper stopped him.

"If anyone could figure out how to beat the odds, it's Tony," she said. "If it was you over there, he'd be finding a way to get you back."

Rhodey moved close to Pepper so that no one else could possibly hear him. "That's just what I am going to do," he said. "You can't tell anyone this, but I'm going back to Afghanistan—and I'm not coming home without him."

Pepper smiled. "Maybe you are Tony's best friend after all."

Rhodey stood on the tarmac at Edwards Air Force Base, a duffel bag slung over his shoulder, waiting in a line of soldiers. Everyone in line saluted as General Gabriel pulled up in a golf cart.

"What do you think you're doing, Rhodes?" Gabriel barked.

"Going back there, sir," Rhodey replied.

The general shook his head. "Listen, son, it's been three months without a single indication that Stark is still alive. We can't keep risking assets—least of all you."

"Are you blocking my transfer, sir?" Rhodey asked.

General Gabriel gazed down the line of soldiers. "Any one of these guys would kill for your career, Rhodes," he said. "Are you telling me you're willing to sacrifice that to fly desert patrol halfway around the world?"

"I am, sir."

The general took a deep breath. "Then I have only one thing to say. Godspeed." He saluted.

Rhodey saluted back and climbed aboard the plane.

Tony finished adjusting the carefully positioned tinsel strips and the laser in the tiny boxlike device. He checked the camera in the corner, remaining out of sight as he worked. It had been difficult to disguise what he and

Yinsen had been doing over the past weeks. This device would make it easier.

He peered through the hole in the front of the box. Inside was a perfect camera-obscura style projection of the lab, with the furnace flickering in the darkness.

Taking a deep breath, Tony crept beneath the surveillance camera, and pushed the box into position. To anyone watching, it would appear as though the lab was quiet, and both men were sleeping. They could only use the box for brief periods before its batteries needed recharging, but hopefully that would buy them enough time to do their secret work.

Tony pulled back his shirt, revealing the glowing Repulsor Technology "heart" keeping him alive. He plugged a long wire into the chest plate and then attached a sensor on the end of the wire to his leg.

Yinsen positioned an electronic contraption that looked like a piece of hinged metal on a tabletop nearby. He nodded and held his breath.

Tony flexed his leg. The glow of his chest plate, which was powering the device, dimmed slightly. The beat-up laptop attached to the device whirred, making the necessary control calculations.

The contraption on the table jumped, moving in the exact same way that Tony's leg had.

The two men looked at each other, triumphant.

Tony unplugged the device. "We're ready," he said. "A week of assembly and we're a go."

"Then perhaps it's time we settle another matter," Yinsen said.

Tony nodded and switched off the hologram projector.

Soon, he and Yinsen sat across the lab table from each other, playing backgammon while they ate. "Yinsen, you've never told me where you're from," Tony said.

Yinsen paused and moved his piece on the board. "I come from a small village not far from here," he said. "It was a good place...before these men ruined it."

"Do you have a family?"

"When I get out of here, I am going to see them again," Yinsen said. "Do you have family, Stark?"

"No."

Yinsen leaned back in his chair. "You're a man who has everything...and nothing."

Without warning, the viewing slat on the door opened, and Abu Bakar stormed in.

Yinsen pointed to a pile of neatly folded laundry,

stacked near the washer and dryer that Tony had demanded as part of his working bargain, and said something in Urdu. Abu Bakar grabbed his laundry, lifted it to his nose, sniffed, and smiled. He walked back to the door, pausing only long enough to sneer at the two men.

"Yeah, yeah," Tony said. "Enjoy your laundry." He and Yinsen turned back to their game.

In Raza's control room, Khalid watched the monitor nervously. On the screen, Yinsen worked furiously, cutting and welding. Sparks flew, at times obscuring the camera's view.

Raza entered the control room and glanced at the monitor. "Khalid," he said, "where is Stark?"

With a shock, Khalid realized that he hadn't seen Stark in some time. It was too early in the day for Tony to be sleeping. He tapped the monitor, as though that might somehow make Stark appear.

"Go find out," Raza growled.

Khalid rushed down the hall to the laboratory door and opened the viewing slat. Inside, Yinsen continued to work furiously. Stark was still nowhere in sight.

"Yinsen!" Khalid called. "Yinsen!"

But Yinsen didn't turn away from his work. Khalid's stomach lurched. Yinsen and Stark were up to something.

He fumbled with the keys, unlocked the door, and pulled it open.

As he did, an explosion rocked the hallway, blasting him back against the wall and knocking him unconscious.

Yinsen waved the smoke from the explosion away from his face. "How'd that work?" Tony asked.

"Oh my goodness," Yinsen said. "It worked all right."

"That's what I do," Tony said. "Come over here and button me up." Tony studied the laptop control screen. They had initialized the power start-up sequence and he watched the laptop screen they were using to monitor it. The program bars were all moving slowly. Too slowly. It was time to get moving.

Yinsen pressed a control button on the lab's winch and lowered a huge metal chest piece over Tony. Stark connected the armor's electronics as Yinsen used a power drill to seal him inside the suit.

Yinsen looked at the laptop. The control bars signaling

the power initialization continued moving very slowly. They could hear the guards outside.

"Get to your cover," Tony said, his voice echoing inside the metal suit. "Remember the checkpoints—make sure each one is clear before you follow me out."

"Sorry, Stark," Yinsen said. "They're coming and you're not ready to go yet. If I can just buy you a few minutes more..."

He turned and ran into the hallway, scooping up Khalid's weapon from the floor.

"Yinsen!" Tony called.

But it was too late. Yinsen ran into the hall, firing the machine gun, trying to keep the guards back.

"Yinsen!" Tony called again, but his friend didn't reply.

Tony looked at the program bars on the laptop, but they were still moving so slowly. Gunfire sounded in the corridor outside. He could hear men running toward the lab.

Now! He needed the programs to finish now!

Suddenly, power surged and the lights dimmed into darkness. Two guards rushed in, firing. Tony grabbed them with his armored hands and threw them aside. As he approached the door, he saw his reflection in the shaving mirror on the wall.

He was huge and bulky, like a walking tank. Crude

gray metal armor covered him from head to toe. The Repulsor Technology generator glowed softly in his chest plate.

He'd become like the prince in Yinsen's story—a man of iron.

As more guards raced into the hall beyond the lab, Iron Man crashed through the doorway.

CHAPTER 7

The guards in the hall fired their weapons. Iron Man surged forward, bullets ricocheting off his armor. His heavy feet pounded the floor, shaking dust from the tunnel ceiling.

Seeing that their bullets had no effect, the guards jumped on him, trying to drag him down. Iron Man tossed them aside: The powerful motors in his armor gave him great strength.

Through the faceplate of his visor, Tony saw—in the distance—light from the cave exit. He lumbered forward, knocking guards out of his way as he went. An insurgent jumped out of a side passage and fired at point-blank range. Iron Man's armor dented, but the bullet still bounced off. He batted the guard aside.

More guards appeared before him, and then more still. Iron Man kept moving, picking up speed like a freight train. He plowed through the enemy, knocking them down like tenpins.

The constant hail of bullets was taking its toll, though. Tony felt the armor bending and weakening around him. Smoke rose from the suit's seams. Tony knew he needed to escape before the suit sustained more damage.

The tunnel opened up into a wide cavern, the main chamber of the complex. The exit beckoned on the other side, but between it and Tony stood a dozen of Raza's men. Yinsen lay crumpled on the ground near the exit, wounded.

Raza's men raised their weapons.

"Look out!" Yinsen cried.

Iron Man turned just in time. A rocket-propelled grenade whizzed past his shoulder and exploded against the wall behind him. The wall crumbled and clouds of dust and smoke filled the room.

Iron Man thumped across the room and knelt awkwardly at his friend's side. Yinsen's wounds looked very bad.

"Why did you run out before we were ready?" Tony asked. "We could have made it—both of us. You could have seen your family again."

A weak smile cracked Yinsen's blackened face. "I'm going to see them again," he said. "They're waiting for me."

In an instant, Tony understood. Yinsen's family was already dead—and Yinsen would soon join them.

"Don't..." Tony began, but it was too late.

Yinsen's eyes closed, and he slumped to the floor.

Rage filled Tony as he rose to his feet. Through the debris, Tony spotted Raza, holding the grenade launcher. The warlord smiled and calmly loaded another grenade. Iron Man whirled on Raza, activating the flamethrowers that were built into his armor. Flames shot out of his hands toward the warlord.

Raza screamed and ducked for cover, dropping the launcher. The weapon exploded as the flames hit it, and part of the tunnel collapsed around the warlord. Iron Man spun toward the exit and turned on the flamethrowers again. The guards blocking his way ran. He screamed as he barreled down the tunnel and out the side of the mountain. As he emerged, the warlord's men kept firing, denting and tearing tiny pieces off Tony's armor.

Iron Man surged forward, heading for the ammunition dump. A maze of boxes, all packed to the brim with weaponry, filled the valley.

Iron Man thundered into the maze. The boxes towered around him—enough armaments to start a war. Tony's eyes stung as he saw the Stark Industries logo emblazoned on the weapon crates. He fired his flamethrowers, and the boxes exploded in flames.

Raza's men followed him in, shooting as they came. The bullets ripped into Iron Man's armor. One caught on a seam and slammed into Tony's shoulder, knocking him off his feet.

His armor moved slowly and the joints ground together as Iron Man rose. Weapon crates burned all around now, but Raza's men didn't seem to care; they wanted to bring Iron Man down for good.

Tony knew the suit couldn't take much more—pieces were already beginning to rattle loose.

He fired one last flame at the weapon crates, then opened a metal flap on the armor's right arm. He flipped the switch inside and a screeching jet engine–like whir filled the maze. The remaining guards covered their ears and fled.

Tony blasted off, soaring into the air like a rocket. As

he went, the ammo dump began to explode—first one crate, then another, and then another, until the whole thing went up in flames.

Sweating, battered, and bruised, Tony concentrated on flying. He shot through the sky like a human cannonball. The desert streaked past below him, the scenery becoming a blur of speed and motion.

He thought he saw something in the distance. Were they helicopters? Were Raza's men still chasing him?

Then, suddenly, his jet boots gave out.

Tony plunged toward the sand, trying desperately to control his flight, but it was no use. He hit hard, spinning and rolling as he plowed into the ground. Pieces of his armor shredded off as he went. Finally, he skidded to a halt. The Iron Man armor was heavy against his skin.

He looked at his chest plate. The Arc generator glowed very faintly. If he used much more of its energy, his heart would stop. Tony cut the power to the suit and slowly, painfully, dragged himself out of the shredded armor. Behind him, explosions from the ammo dump echoed like distant thunder.

He had to keep moving. Raza's men would be after him.

He staggered to his feet, leaving the shredded armor

behind, and limped across the desert, away from Raza's camp. His shoulder ached where the bullet had hit him. He clutched the wound, trying to stop the bleeding.

Don't pass out, he told himself. *Don't pass out.*

He kept walking for as long as he could. But soon he couldn't go any farther. He hadn't eaten, or slept, or had any water since leaving the camp. "Should have thought of bringing supplies," he told himself as the sun beat down on him.

He closed his eyes to try to block out the glare, but his eyelids didn't want to open again. Something pounded in his ears.

High above him he spotted a helicopter. The sound was very close, almost on top of him. He tried to run, but his legs wouldn't move.

His strength gave out, and he slumped blindly toward the sand. A pair of strong arms caught him. "Hey," a familiar voice said. "How was the Fun-Vee?"

Tony's eyes flickered open and he looked up. It was Rhodey.

"Next time, you ride with me, okay?" he said.

"About time you got here," Tony muttered through parched lips.

CHAPTER 8

ays later, the air force C-17 transport carrying Tony
back to the United States touched down on the run-
way at Edwards Air Force Base. Tony, who was seated
in a wheelchair, waited beside Rhodey as the plane's rear
ramp descended.

As Rhodey wheeled his friend off the plane, Tony
spotted Pepper standing near the terminal. "Help me out
of this thing," Tony said. He struggled to his feet and
Rhodey steadied him.

"I got you, pal," Rhodey said.

Together they walked to where Pepper waited, standing beside Tony's limousine.

"Thank you," Pepper said to Rhodey.

Rhodey smiled.

Tony took a deep breath as Pepper turned toward him. He didn't need to see the sympathy on her face to know how bad he looked. He was not the same man he'd been before Raza captured him—he would never be.

"Your eyes are red," Tony said to her. "A few tears for your long-lost boss?"

"Tears of joy," she replied. "I hate job hunting."

Pepper helped Tony into the limo and then climbed in herself.

"Where to, Mr. Stark?" Happy asked, hopping behind the wheel.

"We're due at the hospital," Pepper said.

"No," Tony replied. "To the office. I've been held captive for three months. There are two things I want to do. I want an American cheeseburger, and the other…" He paused when he saw Pepper giving him a look. "Is not what you think. I want you to call a press conference."

53

A huge group of employees, including Obadiah Stane, had gathered outside the main office tower at the campus headquarters of Stark Industries. They burst into applause as Tony's limo pulled up.

Pepper looked at her boss, worried, and helped him get out of the car.

Stane stepped forward and embraced Tony in a bear hug.

"Welcome home, boss," he said. Then, more quietly, so only Tony and Pepper could hear, he added, "I thought we were meeting at the hospital. There are a lot of reporters here, waiting for you. What's going on?"

"You'll see," Tony said.

Tony leaned on Stane's shoulder, and the two of them walked into the building's main entrance. Pepper followed. Reporters packed the lobby from wall to wall.

Pepper didn't notice the man in the dark, tailored suit until he walked up behind her. He was tall, around forty, with a stern face and impeccably groomed hair.

"You'll have to take a seat, sir," Pepper said distractedly.

"I'm not a reporter," the man replied. "I'm Agent Phil Coulson, with the Strategic Homeland Intervention, Enforcement, and Logistics Division."

"That's a mouthful," Pepper said, her eyes not leaving Tony for a moment.

"I know," Coulson said, handing her his business card.

Pepper barely glanced at it. "Look, Mr. Coulson," she said, "we've already spoken with the DOD, the FBI, the CIA, the—"

"We're a separate division with a more...specific focus," Coulson said. "We need to debrief Tony about the circumstances of his escape."

"Well, that's great," Pepper said, cutting him off. "I'll let him know when he's got a free moment."

"We're here to help," Coulson insisted. "I assure you, Mr. Stark will want to talk to us."

"I'm sure he will," Pepper said. "Now, if you could just take your seat."

She walked away from the agent, moving through the crowd toward the podium. Tony looked shaky as he made his way to the microphones. Stane stayed by his side, ready to catch his boss if he staggered.

Tony sat in front of the podium eating his cheese-burger. "Hey, would it be all right if everyone sat down?" he said to the reporters. With some puzzled looks, they did. Then before Stane could step in, he cleared his throat and got started.

"I..." Tony began, "I never got to say good-bye to my father. There're questions I would have asked him. I would have asked him how he felt about what this company did. If he was ever conflicted, if he ever had any doubts...or maybe he was every inch the man we all remember from the newsreels." Tony paused and then went on. "I saw young Americans killed by the very weapons I created to defend them. And I saw that I had become part of a system that is comfortable with zero accountability."

Reporters shouted questions over each other. Finally, one voice rose above the rest.

"Mr. Stark," a reporter said. "What exactly happened to you over there?"

Tony looked thoughtful for a moment, and then all his emotions seemed to overflow.

"What happened over there?" he repeated. "I had my eyes opened. I came to realize that I have more to offer this world than just making things that blow up. And that is why, effective immediately, I am shutting down the weapons manufacturing division of Stark Industries."

In the pandemonium that followed this thunderbolt of an announcement, Rhodey sidled up to Pepper. "Weren't we taking him to the hospital?" he asked. She shrugged.

Onstage next to Tony, Obadiah Stane's jaw dropped, and the lobby erupted into chaos. Stane moved to cut Tony off.

"We've lost our way," Tony continued. "I need to re-evaluate things. And my heart is telling me that I have more to offer the planet than blowing things up."

Tony put his arm around the flustered-looking Stane. "In the coming months," Tony said, "Mr. Stane and I will set a new course for Stark Industries. 'Tomorrow Today' has always been our slogan. It's time we try to live up to it."

Reporters shouted questions as Tony stepped back and Stane took the podium.

"Okay," Stane said. "What we should take away from this is that Tony's back, he's healthier than ever, and as soon as he heals up and takes some time off, we're going to have a little internal discussion and get back to you. Thank you for coming by."

Tony stepped off the stage, beaming. Pepper had never seen him so enthusiastic. He quickly worked his way through the crowd to where she and Rhodey were standing.

"Do you mean that?" Pepper asked.

"Wait and see," Tony replied. He headed out the side door and into the company's sprawling campus.

Stane found him near the Arc Reactor building. "That went well," Stane said sarcastically.

"Did I just paint a target on the back of my head?" Tony asked.

"The back of your head?" Stane replied. "What about the back of my head? How much do you think our stock is going to drop tomorrow?"

Tony thought a moment. "Forty points."

"Minimum," Stane said, concerned. "Tony, we are a weapons manufacturer."

"I don't want a body count to be our only legacy," Tony said.

Stane frowned at him. "What we do here keeps the world from falling into chaos."

"Well, judging from what I've seen," Tony said, "we're not doing a very good job. There are other things we can do."

"Like what?" Stane asked. "You want us to make baby bottles?"

"We could reopen development of Arc Reactor tech," Tony mused.

"The Arc Reactor was a publicity stunt," Stane said. "We built it to shut up the hippies."

"It works," Tony observed.

"Yeah, as a science project," Stane replied. "It was never cost-effective. We knew that before we built it. Repulsor Arc Reactor Technology is a dead end. Right?"

"Maybe," Tony replied.

Stane looked at him anxiously. "There haven't been any breakthroughs in thirty years. Right?"

Tony shook his head. "You're a lousy poker player, Obadiah. Who told you?"

"Come on," Stane said with a big grin, like they already were sharing a secret. "Let me see the thing."

"Was it Rhodey?" Tony asked.

"Just show it to me," Stane said.

Tony ripped open his shirt, revealing the glowing electronic unit in the middle of his chest.

"Well," Stane said, marveling. He took a deep breath. "Listen, we're a team. There's nothing we can't do if we stick together. No more of this ready-fire-aim business. No more unplanned press conferences. Can you promise me that?"

"Maybe," Tony said.

Stane straightened up. "Let me handle this," he said. "I did it for your father; I'll do it for you, but, please, you just have to lie low for a while."

But "lying low" was never something Tony Stark was good at.

CHAPTER 9

The Stark mansion came alive as Tony walked through
the door. Jarvis, the house's computer system, turned
on the lights, changed the color of the windows, switched
the TV to Tony's favorite channel, and adjusted everything to Tony's preprogrammed preferences.

"Hello, Mr. Stark," said Jarvis's almost-human voice.

"Hello, Jarvis," Tony replied.

"What can I do for you, sir?"

"I need to build a better heart," Tony said.

"I'm not sure I follow, sir."

"Give me a scan and you'll see what I mean," Tony replied.

"Shall I prepare the scanner in the workshop, sir?" Jarvis asked.

"Please. I'll need a full analysis."

Less than twenty minutes later, Tony sat in the scanning booth in his lab. Laser beams and ultrasound imagers flashed over Tony's body, analyzing him from head to toe.

"State your intentions for the RT device in your chest, sir," Jarvis said.

"It powers an electromagnet that keeps shrapnel from entering my heart," Tony replied. "Can you recommend any upgrades?"

"Why are you talking to me like a computer?" Jarvis asked, his electronic voice betraying not a hint of irony.

"Because you're acting like one," Tony replied. "I remember you having more personality than this."

"Should I activate sarcasm harmonics?"

"Fine. Could you please make your recommendations now?"

"It would thrill me to no end," Jarvis said.

A smile tugged at the corners of Tony's mouth. "Ah. That's more like it."

"Would you like them on-screen, or shall I talk for the next three-point-two hours?"

"On-screen would be great," Tony said.

A series of recommendations and schematics appeared on the lab's monitors. Tony studied them quickly, his keen mind taking in every detail.

"Great," he said. "Perfect. Just what I had in mind."

"Of course, sir," Jarvis said. "Shall I begin machining the parts?"

Tony loaded raw metal stock into the lab's machine-tool facilities and watched as Jarvis began cutting.

Half a world away, in the deserts of Afghanistan, a swarm of ragged men scoured the sand dunes, looking for items to scavenge.

"Over here! I found something!" one man called, pointing to a battered gauntlet protruding from the sand. He tugged the metal glove free and held it high, as though it were a trophy.

A corroded pickup truck bounced over the dunes toward the discovery. In the back of the truck stood a powerful man holding a mounted machine gun. A banner showing ten conjoined rings fluttered over the machine gunner's head.

The truck pulled up next to the discoverer and he threw the gauntlet into the back. He smiled up at the machine gunner's scarred and burned face, hoping for approval.

Raza, the scarred man, merely nodded.

"There's more here!" cried a man atop another dune.

"And here!" called another, farther on.

Raza picked up Iron Man's battered helmet from the truck bed and stared into the helmet's empty eye sockets. "Keep looking," he called to his men. "Bring me every piece of armor you find—no matter how small. I want all of it."

Pepper hung up on Agent Coulson for the third time— he was getting to be a real pest—and knocked on Tony's bedroom door. When no one answered, she poked her head inside. The bed was made but not slept in, though the TV was on. A finance advice show blared news about Stark Industries.

"I have one recommendation," the moderator was saying. "Sell! Abandon ship." Behind him, the day's newspaper headlines blazed across the screen—STARK RAVING MAD?, STARK LUNACY, and other similar rants.

When Tony's voice came over the bedroom intercom, Pepper jumped. "Pepper, how big are your hands?" he asked.

Frowning, she hurried through the security doors and down to Tony's lab. When she arrived, she found the workshop dimly lit, dirty, and disorganized. Tony was sitting in a chair, shirtless, his chest plate glowing slightly.

Pepper steeled herself. Though she knew the device implanted in his chest had saved Tony's life, she still hadn't gotten used to it.

"I need you to help me," Tony said.

She stared at the glowing Repulsor Tech device in his chest. "So that's the thing that's keeping you alive."

"That's the thing that was keeping me alive," he said. "It's now an antique. This is what will be keeping me alive for the foreseeable future." He held up a similar device that looked much more high-tech and powerful.

"Amazing," she said.

"I'm going to swap them out and switch all functions to the new unit," Tony said.

"Is it safe?" Pepper asked.

"Completely," he assured her. "First, I need you to reach in and—"

"Reach in to where?" she asked warily.

"The socket in my chest," Tony said. "Listen carefully, because we have to do this in a matter of minutes."

"Or else what?"

"I could go into cardiac arrest," Tony replied.

Pepper's stomach twisted into a knot. "I thought you said it was safe."

"I didn't want you to panic."

She felt the blood drain from her face.

"Stay with me," Tony said. "I'm going to lift off the old chest piece—"

"That won't kill you?"

"Not immediately. When I lift it off, I need you to reach into the socket...." Tony kept talking, giving quick but complete directions so she could replace the unit.

Somehow, Pepper managed to get through the procedure without passing out. Afterward, she gazed at the old "heart" while one of the lab's robot arms finished installing the new unit.

"Can I wash my hands now?" she asked.

"Sure," he said, continuing to talk as she went to the sink. "The new unit is much more efficient. This shouldn't happen again."

"Good," she said, drying off, "because it's not in my job description."

"It is now," Tony replied.

She frowned at him and picked up the old unit. "What should I do with this?" she asked. The tiny power plant glowed slightly in her hand.

"That old thing?" Tony replied. "Throw it out."

Pepper frowned. "You made it out of spare parts in a dungeon. It saved your life. Doesn't it at least have some nostalgic value?"

"Pepper," Tony said, "I have been called many things, but nostalgic is not one of them." The robot finished the installation of the new unit; the center of Tony's chest glowed brightly.

"There," Tony said. "Good as new. Thank you."

"You're welcome," Pepper said, feeling greatly relieved. "Can I ask you a favor? If you need someone to do something like this again," she said, "get someone else."

"I don't have anyone else," Tony replied.

He looked into her eyes and, for a moment, she felt something for him she'd never felt before. She turned away. "Will that be all, Mr. Stark?"

"That will be all, Ms. Potts."

CHAPTER 10

B efore he went further with his new project, Tony felt like he had to set a couple of things straight with Rhodey. He caught his army pal in the midst of a presentation, where Rhodey was arguing that the air force would always need pilots. "No unmanned aerial vehicle will ever trump a pilot's instinct, his insight, his ability to look into a situation beyond the obvious and discern its outcome... or his judgment."

"Colonel?" Tony called out. "Why not a pilot without the plane?"

Rhodey saw him and rolled his eyes. "Give us a couple

minutes, guys," he said, and started walking with Tony. "Didn't expect to see you around so soon," he said.

"Rhodey, I'm working on something big," Tony said. "I want you to be part of it."

"You're about to make a lot of people around here real happy," Rhodey said, thinking Tony was talking about a new military project.

"This is not for the military," Tony said. "I'm not…it's different."

"What, you're a humanitarian now or something?" Rhodey asked.

Nobody believed Tony had actually had a change of heart. "I need you to listen to me," he said.

"No," Rhodey cut him off. "What you need is time to get your mind right. I'm serious."

Tony knew people, and he knew when he wasn't going to get anywhere by arguing. "Okay," he said, taking a step back. He had hoped to show the new project to Rhodey so his friend would understand, but Rhodey was still thinking like a soldier.

That was part of the problem Tony wanted to fix.

Sketches and designs lay scattered across the worktable in Tony's lab as he tinkered with his newest invention—a pair of shining metal boots. "Jarvis, you up?"

"For you, sir, always."

"I'd like to open a new project file, index as Mark Two. Until further notice, why don't we just keep everything on my private server?"

"Working on a secret project, are we, sir?"

"Don't want this ending up in the wrong hands," Tony said. "Maybe in mine, it can actually do some good."

"Still having trouble walking, sir?" Jarvis asked.

"These aren't for walking," Tony replied.

He finished the adjustments, put the boots down, and marked a circle on the lab floor with electrical tape.

"Why are you marking up the floor?" the computerized butler asked.

"It's a test circle," Tony replied. "It'll help me gauge the experiment's success."

"I'll inform the cleaning staff," Jarvis said.

Tony put on the boots and stepped to the center of the circle. He draped a bandolier-like control device around his shoulders and hooked it all into his chest unit.

"Ready to record the big moment, Jarvis?" he asked, gripping the bandolier's joystick controls.

"All sensors ready, sir."

"We'll start off easy," Tony said. "Ten percent power." He pressed the activators on the joysticks.

The boot jets fired and he shot toward the ceiling. He wrestled with the controls, flipped sideways, barely avoided the ceiling, and careened around the workshop before finally crashing into the wall and falling into a pile of cardboard boxes in the corner.

As Tony lay upside down amid mounds of plastic packing material, Jarvis said, "That flight yielded excellent data, sir."

"Great," Tony replied.

Days later, Pepper came into the workshop as Tony fiddled with a pair of metal gauntlets. He put the gloves on, pointed them across the lab, and activated the Repulsor Technology pads in the palms.

A blast of light issued forth from his hands. It hit a toolbox fifteen feet away, knocking it over and scattering the wrenches inside across the floor.

Pepper frowned. "I thought you were done inventing weapons," she said.

"It's not a weapon," Tony replied. "It's a flight stabilizer."

"Well, watch where you're pointing your flight stabilizer, would you?"

He gave a sheepish grin.

"Obadiah's upstairs," she said. "Should I tell him you're in?"

"I'll be right up," Tony replied.

As she left, she placed a small box on the edge of his worktable. Intrigued, Tony took off the gauntlets and ripped the package open.

Inside was his old chest device, encased in shatterproof plastic. The reactor glowed faintly inside the clear material. Tony knew it would continue to glow for years. The casing had an inscription: PROOF THAT TONY STARK HAS A HEART. Tony chuckled and headed upstairs.

He reached the living room just as Obadiah Stane set a pizza down on the coffee table. Stane flashed the billionaire a concerned smile. "It went that bad, huh?" Tony asked.

"Just because I brought pizza from New York doesn't mean it went bad," Stane said. Then, after a pause, he added, "It would have gone better if you were there."

"You told me to lie low," Tony said. "That's what I've been doing. I lie low and you take care of all..."

Stane nodded, appearing genuinely touched. He took a deep breath, too. "Come on," he said. "In public, sure. The press. But this was a board of directors meeting?"

"It was?"

"The board is claiming you have post-traumatic stress. They're filing an injunction."

Tony's jaw dropped. "What?"

"They want to lock you out."

Tony began pacing again. "How can they do that? It's my name on the building—my ideas that run the company!"

"Well, they're going to try," Stane said. "We'll fight them, of course."

"With the amount of stock we own, I thought we controlled the company," Tony said.

Stane shook his head. "Tony, the board has rights, too. They're making the case that you and your new direction isn't in the company's best interests."

Tony was working up a good fury against the board. "This is great," he said, and turned away from Obie. "I'll be in the shop."

"Hey, hey! Tony, listen. I'm trying to turn this thing around, but you have to give me something." Obie came closer to Tony and tapped the RT in his chest. "Let me have the engineers analyze that. You know, draw up some specs."

"Absolutely not," Tony said. "This one stays with me."

Obie looked like he might pursue it, but then he just picked up the pizza. "All right, well, this stays with me, then." He offered Tony a slice.

"Thanks," Tony said.

Good humor between them restored, Stane asked, "Mind if I come down there and see what you're doing?"

"Good night, Obie," Tony said, and went back to the lab.

It took him a few more days to hook the boot units, the control bandolier, and the new gauntlets together. Once he'd done it, though, he couldn't resist trying out the setup.

"Shall I alert the rescue squad?" Jarvis asked as Tony fastened the last of the connections.

Tony flexed his arms. The tubing connecting the pieces felt stiff—but it was only a prototype after all. All he was wearing were the boots and gauntlets, just to try out flight stability. He had one of his lab robots, affectionately named Dummy, on fire control. "If you douse me again and I'm not on fire, I'm donating you to a city college," he warned Dummy, who didn't have a perfect grasp on its duties.

"All right, nice and easy," Tony said. "Just starting with one percent thrust capacity." He activated the boot jets and manipulated the controls.

Slowly, he rose off the floor and hovered in the air. The repulsor stabilizers in the gloves kicked in, steadying his flight. He moved up in the air, holding his arms out like a tightrope walker.

"And let's bring it up to two point five," he said. The surge of energy nearly crashed him into the ceiling, and it took him some flailing around to get the hang of using the gauntlets to keep himself steady while the boots provided life.

After gaining his balance, he floated slowly around the room, dodging expensive pieces of electronic equipment and avoiding the cars, workbench, and other obstacles.

He nearly bumped his head on the ceiling twice and came perilously close to the roof of his Porsche, but he didn't hit anything. His papers and a few light objects scattered out of his way as he flew, repelled by the repulsor forces powering the boots and the gauntlets.

"See?" he said. "Nothing to it."

He cut the propulsion, landed softly near his work-bench, and grinned at one of Jarvis's sensors.

That was when Dummy unloaded on him with the fire extinguisher. "No!" Tony shouted. When Dummy cut off the extinguisher, Tony briefly considered using it as repulsor target practice. Then he changed his mind. After all, he'd just done something incredible. What was a little fire-extinguisher foam? That wasn't going to dampen his mood.

"Yeah," Tony said. "I can fly."

Half a world away, Raza stared at the gray suit of armor being assembled on the lab table in his new hideout.

"Amazing," he muttered. Amazing that something like this could nearly destroy his whole operation.

It would be difficult to complete the reassembly without either Yinsen or Stark to guide his workers, but Raza knew the job would eventually get done.

And then he, Raza, would own a weapon that would be the envy of even the largest corporations and governments.

The warlord smiled and, for once, he did not mind the stiffness of his scarred face.

CHAPTER 11

Tony's metal boots clanked across the workshop floor. The armor felt heavy, so he made an adjustment to the servo-motors that powered it. His Repulsor Technology heart glowed more brightly within his chest plate, and the suit moved more easily.

He flexed his arms and the suit flexed with him. The ailerons, air brakes, and other flying controls popped out on command, just as they were supposed to. The new armor covering him from head to toe felt good.

"Stand by for calibration," he told Jarvis.

"Of course, sir," the computerized butler replied.

Tony fired up the boots and the gauntlet repulsors. He rose into the air, hovered, and began to fly around the workshop. Then, suddenly, he lost his balance and plunged toward the floor.

He landed on his sports car, crushing the roof flat. The car's alarm system screamed in protest. Tony blasted the alarm with the repulsor mounted in his palm. The alarm unit shook to pieces and went silent.

"A not entirely unsuccessful test," Jarvis observed.

Tony picked himself up, brushing stray bits of the automobile off his armor. "We should take this outside," he said.

"I must strongly caution against that," Jarvis warned. "There are terabytes of calculations still needed before the armor is fully operational and under control."

Behind his metal helmet, Tony smiled. "Jarvis, sometimes you have to run before you can walk. We'll do those calculations in flight."

"Sir..." Jarvis said.

"That's why you'll be making the flight with me," Tony replied.

He pressed a button on a lab console and downloaded Jarvis's program into the suit's computer system. The armor's heads-up display flashed to life. "Ready?" Tony said.

"Three…two…one…" The lift jets in the suit's boots fired up. "Handles like a dream," he said.

Tony opened the workshop's garage doors and slowly hovered out the door and along the workshop driveway.

Jarvis's voice echoed in his helmet. "I suggest you allow me to employ Directive Four," the butler said.

Tony frowned, not remembering which directive that was. "Never interrupt me while I'm with a beautiful woman?" he guessed.

"That's Directive Six," Jarvis replied. "Directive Four is to use any and all means to protect your life, should you be incapable of doing so."

"Whatever," Tony replied. "Let's see what this thing can do." He kicked up the power and blasted into the night sky.

Iron Man weaved and wobbled through the air, trying to keep the horizon steady. He tried poses he'd seen in various movies, books, and comics about flying super heroes, but each one seemed more unstable than the previous one.

Then he had an idea. *You're jet powered,* he told himself. *Think like a jet.*

He thrust his chest out, held his chin up, kept his knees and feet together, and flung his arms out to the side—like a delta-winged fighter aircraft.

To his delight, the pose worked, and he zoomed through the air like a human missile. He pulled a few exhilarating banked turns, and then followed the ribbon of the Pacific Coast Highway south to Santa Monica. Onlookers gaped in awe as Iron Man buzzed by the giant Ferris wheel on the pier.

Tony smiled and arced upward in a power climb. The clouds streaked past like misty dreams. Soon he emerged into a perfect, starry night.

He was so high up now that the world seemed a tiny, distant place. Ice crystals formed on the inside of his helmet.

"Sir, there is a potentially fatal buildup of ice occurring," Jarvis warned.

Caught up in the moment, Tony didn't listen. Instead, he zoomed ever higher, chasing the stars.

"Mr. Stark," Jarvis said, "please acknowledge."

The moon beckoned before him, huge and impossibly bright. Tony never remembered seeing anything more beautiful in his life.

Suddenly, the heads-up display inside Tony's helmet went dark. One remaining warning light flashed: SYSTEM SHUTDOWN.

"We iced up, Jarvis!" Tony shouted. "Deploy flaps! Jarvis!"

But the shutdown had taken Jarvis off-line as well.

Iron Man's thrusters sputtered and died. The suit felt heavy and awkward. Tony glanced at his chest plate; it wasn't glowing.

The weight of the armor overcame his momentum and he plummeted, pinwheeling toward the earth.

"Uh, Jarvis?" Tony called. "Jarvis!"

The earth zoomed up toward him.

"Status!" Tony called to the silent computer system. "Status! Reboot!"

He plummeted through the clouds. The coastline appeared below, the lights of the city blazed into view, and the snaking curve of the highway revealed itself.

Why hadn't he listened to Jarvis?

Something popped near his ear and, suddenly, the heads-up display flickered back to life. Power surged through the suit's servo-motors and circuits. Tony fought to bring the armor back under control.

"Temporary power restored," Jarvis said calmly. "Descend immediately."

Tony righted himself and flew back toward the mansion. He aimed for the driveway, struggling to maintain stability.

"Shall I take over the final descent?" Jarvis asked.

"No," Tony said proudly. "I've got it. I—"

An accidental shift of his weight sent him crashing through the roof of the mansion.

Shattered beams and plaster rained around him as he broke through the ceiling of his garage and landed on top of another sports car, wrecking his piano on the way through the living room.

The impact shook his entire body and set off every car alarm in the garage. The robot he called Dummy sprayed him with a fire extinguisher. Annoyed, Tony said, "Kill power." The suit went dark again. He scrambled to his feet and pulled off his helmet.

"Shall I alert the body shop, sir?" Jarvis asked.

"No," Tony replied. "Just switch the alarms off and let security know we've had a little ... setback."

"Very good, sir," Jarvis said.

He clambered out of the armor and hung it on the work rack nearby, then began typing design notes into his computer. Graphics and data scrolled down the lab's many monitors.

"Notes," Tony said, getting right to work. "Main transducer felt sluggish at plus forty altitude. Hull pressurization is problematic. I think the icing might have been a factor."

"This design isn't rated for high altitude," Jarvis observed. "You're expending eight percent power just heating and pressurizing."

"Reconfigure the suit using the gold-titanium alloy from the Seraphim Tactical Satellite. It should ensure fuselage integrity to fifty thousand feet while still maintaining power-to-weight ratio."

"Shall I simulate a new hull utilizing the proposed specifications on-screen?" Jarvis asked.

"Thrill me."

On-screen, the sleek form of the Mark II armor transformed into an even sleeker golden Mark III prototype.

Tony regarded it and rubbed his chin. "A bit...ostentatious, isn't it?" He glanced over at his collection of cars and motorcycles, seeking inspiration in their paint jobs.

"Add a little red, would you?" he said, pointing to the screen. "Here, here, and here." The computer graphics prototype changed color appropriately.

Just then, Tony noticed the image on the television, which had been playing silently in the background. He turned up the volume.

A local reporter stood outside a grand entertainment hall where a huge crowd was gathering. "Tonight's red-hot red carpet is here at the Concert Hall, where Tony

Stark's annual benefit for the Firefighters' Family Fund has become the go-to charity gala on LA's high-society calendar."

"Jarvis, we get an invite for that?" Tony asked.

"I have no record of an invitation, sir," Jarvis replied.

Nearby, the lab's automated tooling and manufacturing machines sprang to life.

"But this great cause is only part of the story," the reporter continued. "The man whose name graces the gold-lettered invitations to the event hasn't been seen in public since his highly controversial press conference. Some say Stark is suffering from post-traumatic stress disorder and hasn't left his bed in weeks."

Tony scoffed and returned his attention to the design screen. The red-and-gold Iron Man Mark III uniform looked good—very good.

"Estimated completion time is five hours," Jarvis noted.

"Good," Tony said. He suddenly had a place to be, and he was very curious why he hadn't been invited in the first place. "Don't wait up for me, honey," he joked, and hurried to get ready.

CHAPTER 12

The crowd outside the concert hall filled the entire avenue and overflowed into the surrounding streets. The concertgoers were a mix of celebrities, generals, business tycoons, and movie stars.

Flashbulbs lit the scene as Tony pulled his sports car up to the curb. He got out, waved to the crowd, and handed his keys to the waiting valet.

The crowd roared as Tony stepped onto the red carpet and, for just a moment, the former prisoner of war felt completely out of place. Not so long ago, these had been his people, but now they were just a sea of faces. There was Obadiah, mixing with the crowd and giving some kind of statement. In other words, grandstanding as usual.

"What's the world coming to when a guy's got to crash his own party?" Tony asked. Stane looked uneasy. He nodded to the other guests. "I'll see you inside," he said, and steered Tony away from the crowd.

"Let's just take it slow, okay?" Stane said. "I've got the board right where we want them." He nodded toward a group of Stark Industries executives milling around with the red-carpet crowd.

"You got it," Tony replied, giving the board members a curt wave. "Just cabin fever. Look, I'll see you inside." He headed for the theater doors, anxious not to get caught up in company business.

The interior of the venue was almost as crowded as outside. Music filled the concert hall as happy couples whirled around the dance floor. Tony spotted Pepper coming down the stairs. She looked stunning in a classic evening gown.

Tony started to head in her direction, but he was interrupted by…what was his name? The guy who had been in the house the other day. "Mr. Stark?" he asked, and introduced himself again. "Agent Coulson."

"Oh yeah," Tony said. "The guy from the…" Again

his memory failed him. The organization with the really long name.

"Strategic Homeland Intervention, Enforcement, and Logistics Division," Coulson said helpfully.

"You need a new name for that," Tony said.

Coulson nodded. "I hear that a lot. Listen, I know this must be a trying time for you, but we need to debrief you. There're still a lot of unanswered questions, and time can be a factor with these things. Let's just put something on the books. How about the twenty-fourth at seven p.m. at Stark Industries?"

"Tell you what," Tony said. "You got it. You're absolutely right." Coulson looked surprised. Tony nodded in Pepper's direction. "Well, I'm going to go to my assistant, and we'll make a date."

As he said it, he finally broke away and caught up to Pepper. She looked surprised and pleased to see him.

"Ms. Potts," Tony said, "can I have five minutes? You look...like you should always wear that dress."

"Thanks," she said. "It was a birthday present—from you."

"I have great taste," Tony said. "Care to dance?" He took her hand and whisked her onto the dance floor. She looked away from him bashfully.

"I'm sorry," Tony said. "Am I making you uncomfortable?"

"No," she replied, her face slightly flushed. "I always wear a chiffon dress, forget to put on deodorant, and dance with my boss in front of everyone I've ever worked with."

"Would it help if I fired you?" Tony asked.

She grinned. "You wouldn't last a week without me."

"I might," Tony said.

"What's your Social Security number?" she asked.

"Uh..." Tony began.

She whispered it into his ear.

Tony chuckled. "I guess I wouldn't make it on my own after all."

They danced together long enough that Tony lost track of time. Finally, they retired to the veranda outside to catch their breath. Pepper looked beautiful in the starlight.

They stood silently for a moment. "That was totally weird," Pepper said after a while.

"Totally harmless," Tony said. "We're dancing. No one's even watching."

"No, it was not just a dance," Pepper said. "You don't understand because you're you. You're my boss, and I'm dancing with you...."

Tony thought he knew what she was saying. It might have seemed a little weird for her to be dancing with the boss, who had a bit of a reputation with the ladies. But it was just a dance. Wasn't it? "I just think you're overstating it," he said.

She shook her head, like he still wasn't getting it. "We're here, and I'm wearing this ridiculous dress, and we're dancing, and then..." Their faces got a little closer together, and Tony realized that if one of them didn't do something they were about to kiss.

Pepper, as usual, was the one who handled the situation. She paused and said, "I would like a drink, please."

"Okay," Tony said.

Tony went and picked up a pair of drinks from the buffet table. Before he could return to Pepper, though, reporter Christine Everhart strode up to him. She had a file folder under her arm.

"Mr. Stark," she said, shoving a microphone into his face, "I was hoping I could get a reaction from you on your company's involvement in this latest atrocity," she said.

"Hey, I didn't set up this event," Tony explained, loosening his collar. "They just put my name on the invitation to draw more people."

She opened the file folder and thrust it toward him. "Is this what you call accountability? It's a town called Gulmira. Heard of it?" Inside the folder were pictures of Ten Rings separatists clutching Stark machine guns, rocket-propelled grenade launchers, and other weapons. Behind them, a village burned.

Tony looked at the photos, and his blood ran cold. "When were these taken?" he asked.

"Yesterday," she replied. "Good public relations move. You tell the world you're a changed man, but continue doing business as usual."

"I didn't approve this shipment," Tony said. He felt as though the world was crumbling around him.

"Well, your company did," Christine replied.

Tony took her by the hand. "Come with me," he said. Together, the two of them strode out of the building to where the huge mass of reporters stood, waiting to take pictures of celebrities leaving the event.

Outpacing Ms. Everhart, Tony saw Obadiah talking to the reporters and made a beeline for him. He thrust the pictures in front of Obadiah, who saw them and immediately hustled Tony away from the reporters. "Please, do you mind?" he growled.

"What's going on in Gulmira?" Tony demanded.

"Tony, Tony," Obadiah said. "You can't afford to be this naive."

"Naive?" Tony said. "When I was growing up, they told me there were lines I couldn't cross because that's how we did business. But in the meantime, Stark Industries is double-dealing under the table. Our company doesn't deserve to represent the United States."

"Tony," Stane said, "you're acting like a child."

Tony gazed into Stane's eyes and saw fear. "You don't believe I can turn this company around," Tony said. "You think we'll go broke unless we sell weapons."

"Tony, you've got about as much control over our business as a child riding in the backseat of your father's car holding a red plastic steering wheel in your hand."

Around them, reporters clamored for pictures, but Tony ignored them. "Maybe I'll just get out of the car," Tony replied.

"You're not even allowed in the car," Stane said. He took a deep breath. "Tony, who do you think locked you out? I was the one who filed the injunction against you."

Tony couldn't believe it. Stane turned and walked away, but Tony caught up to him.

He grabbed Stane by the jacket and spun him around. "Why?" Tony asked angrily.

"It's the only way I could protect you," Stane replied. As he said it, two large bodyguards stepped between him and Tony. With a final shake of his head, Stane left the party and climbed into his waiting limousine.

No, Tony thought. This was not going to be how it worked.

CHAPTER 13

Tony sat hunched over his workbench, wearing a prototype of the Mark III Iron Man gauntlet. On the wall beside him, a large flat-screen TV monitor blared with the latest news.

The TV showed long lines of refugees streaming out of the ruins of Gulmira as triumphant Ten Rings separatists ran rampant through Gulmira City. It seemed that Raza's rebel group was spreading beyond Afghanistan.

Tony aimed the gauntlet at a hanging light fixture twenty feet away and activated the repulsor unit. The lights sparked and fizzled and fell from the ceiling.

The scene on the TV switched, now showing half-starved refugees gathered in makeshift camps and caves in the Gulmira hills. In the midst of the crowd, a starving child wept.

Tony adjusted the gauntlet, raising the power level. He pointed it toward a window on the far side of the lab and fired. The blast shattered the glass and knocked a nearby picture off the wall.

"With no international political will or pressure," the TV reporter concluded, "there is little hope for these newly displaced refugees—refugees who can only wonder one thing: Is the world watching?"

Tony made a final adjustment to the gauntlet and blasted the TV to smithereens. As silence descended over the lab, he nodded in satisfaction. It was time for him to get more closely acquainted with the situation in Gulmira.

The suit was fast. He covered half the world in a few hours and closed in on Gulmira by the next sunrise.

The city was under siege by the same black-clad Ten Rings rebels who had held Tony and Yinsen hostage.

They patrolled among the hovels and refugee tents on the outskirts of the city, gathering the local men of fighting age to hold them hostage.

A boy not more than twelve years old darted through an alleyway, clutching a puppy in his arms. He didn't see the four separatists in the square until he almost ran into them. The men shouted and raised their weapons; the boy cowered, knowing he was doomed.

Iron Man dropped out of the night sky, landing between the rebels and their intended victim. They quickly shielded themselves with hostages, but Tony had anticipated a situation like this when he was putting the finishing touches on the armor's close-range combat systems. Multiple targeting icons appeared in the suit's heads-up display and at a single vocal command, every rebel was dropped by a microslug fired from a tiny turret battery inside the armor housing.

The hostages scattered, and so did the boy.

Tony lifted off again, heading back toward the town, when a missile blew him out of the sky. His armor handled the impact, but his sensors and navigation systems were scrambled for a brief moment. When he had them reset, he locked in on the truck that had fired the missile and destroyed it with a repulsor blast. Then he strode through the Ten Rings encampment and destroyed all the old Stark weaponry he could find, setting off a series of enormous explosions that echoed throughout the valley.

It felt good to settle some scores on Yinsen's behalf, and also to get the local people out from under the tyranny of the Ten Rings. But before Iron Man could enjoy the victory, a tank shell shattered the building next to him. Tony staggered as tons of bricks and mortar rained down on his armor. The refugees, who had crept out of hiding to watch Iron Man, scurried back to safety.

Then the tank itself rumbled into view, knocking down makeshift hovels as it came. It trained its turret cannon toward Iron Man as he rose to his feet.

Tony studied the tank's schematic on his heads-up display. The tank was Stark designed, and his computer files showed him everything about it, including its weaknesses.

The tank fired again, but Iron Man was already moving. A mini missile launcher popped open on Tony's left gauntlet.

Iron Man fired the missile into the tank, hitting it between the body and turret. The tank's systems overloaded, and moments later, its passengers jumped to safety as the tank exploded.

Tony's heads-up display showed someone coming up behind him. He whirled, repulsors ready to blast the enemy into next week.

But it was only a child—the same boy Tony had rescued earlier. In his outstretched hand, the boy held an apple.

Iron Man mussed the boy's hair affectionately and then took to the sky once more. He looked around and saw no more rebels prowling the streets. The refugees below cheered. Heaving a sigh of relief, Tony said, "Jarvis, plot a course for home."

The explosions in Gulmira did not go unnoticed in the air force command center where Colonel James Rhodes was a staff officer. "What was that?" the general wanted to know. "Were we cleared to go in there?"

"We got a bogey!" a surveillance officer announced. "Wasn't air force."

The radar signal was small, very maneuverable, and very fast. "We've got the CIA on the line. They want to know if it's us," the general said.

"No, it definitely is not us. It wasn't navy. Wasn't marines." Various staff officers chimed in.

"Get Colonel Rhodes down here now!" the general commanded.

A minute later, Rhodey walked in and got a quick briefing. "We think it's an unmanned aerial vehicle," one of the officers concluded.

Rhodey thought a moment and then said, "Let me make a call." He picked up a phone and punched in Tony Stark's private number. A moment later, Tony's voice came over the earpiece.

"Yeah?"

Rhodey could barely hear him; it was a terrible connection. "Tony, it's Rhodey. What's that noise?"

"Oh yeah, I'm driving with the top down," Tony replied. "Look, this isn't the best time—"

"I need a quick ID," Rhodey said, studying the ongoing satellite pictures. "We've got a weapons depot that was just blown up a few clicks from where you were being held captive."

"Well, that's a hot spot," Tony said. "Sounds like someone stepped in and did your job for you, huh?"

Rhodey covered the phone's receiver as the control officer said, "The unmanned aerial vehicle has entered the no-fly zone."

"You sure you don't have any tech in that area I should know about?" Rhodey asked.

"Nope. Why do you ask?"

One of the staff officers signaled a patrolling F-22 to approach the bogey. "Whiplash, come in hot," he said.

"Because I think I'm staring at one right now," Rhodey said, "and it's about to get blown to kingdom come."

An alarm blared in the control room, announcing that the unmanned aerial vehicle, called a UAV, was violating the patrolled airspace.

"That's my exit," Tony said. The connection broke with a click.

Tony looked up as two US Air Force F-22 Raptors streaked out of the sky toward him.

The jets screamed ahead, gaining on him. Tony turned on the armor's turbo booster and shot forward. He pulled into a tight bank, but the planes remained on his tail.

Beads of sweat rolled down Tony's back. Every time he turned, the planes turned with him. His heads-up display showed their weapons systems trying to lock on.

He knew it wouldn't be long before they had him in their sights.

But would they fire? He was on their side after all.

The problem was, they didn't know that.

"Pursuing aircraft have locked on," Jarvis announced calmly.

Tony glanced back over his shoulder as the lead jet fired a missile at him.

CHAPTER 14

The missile streaked straight toward Iron Man. In his revamped armor, Tony was as fast as the jets—but the Sidewinder missile was faster still.

Tony concentrated, sending every iota of power he could into the suit's thrusters but, each moment, his heads-up display showed the missile gaining on him.

Jarvis's voice remained calm. "Incoming Sidewinder in five...four...three...two..."

Tony activated the suit's countermeasures. Instantly a hatch popped open, and big, confettilike flakes of metal burst into the air.

The sidewinder hit the chaff and exploded. The fireball from the explosion surrounded Iron Man, but Tony didn't even feel it through the armor.

Unfortunately, the F-22 jets hadn't given up yet.

Iron Man dived toward the ground, rolled to his left, and banked right. The Raptors followed close behind.

Tony flew as fast as he could, trying to keep the jets from locking on again. He banked into a hard turn. The g-force meter inside his helmet went from green to yellow to red. The world around him blurred, and Tony nearly blacked out.

"Sir," Jarvis said, "may I remind you that the suit can handle these maneuvers, but you cannot."

The F-22s sprayed machine-gun fire into Iron Man's path. White-hot tracer rounds streaked past Tony, exploding and ricocheting off his armor. For the first time, the new suit buckled and tore.

Tony grimaced and said, "Jarvis—air brakes!"

Instantly, all of the suit's drag-inducing flaps opened, slowing Iron Man to a halt in seconds. Tony grunted as g-forces pressed him against the inside of the suit.

The jets shot past Iron Man, twin blurs of aviation gray. Tony breathed a sigh of relief. The Raptors would be miles away before they could turn back on him again.

"Jarvis," he said, "get Rhodey on the line."

The computerized butler put the call through.

"Hello?" Rhodey's voice said.

"Hi, Rhodey, it's me. You asked. What you were asking about is me."

"No, see, this isn't a game. You do not send civilian equipment into my active war zone. You understand that?"

"This is not a piece of equipment. I'm in it. It's a suit. It's me!"

"Mark your position and return to base," the commanding officer said.

"Roger that, Ballroom," Whiplash Two said.

"At once, sir."

As the jets screamed past overhead, Iron Man shot up from the ground and clamped onto the belly of the closest one. Unfortunately, it only took a moment for the Raptor's wingman to notice.

"Whiplash One, he's on your belly," the second jet's pilot called.

"What?" Whiplash One asked, seemingly unable to believe it.

"He's clinging to your belly! Shake him off!"

The F-22 Raptor immediately began a series of swoops,

dives, and turns. Even with his armor-enhanced fingers, Tony barely hung on. The maneuvers shook him inside the suit like nails inside a tin can.

"Headquarters," Whiplash Two said, "that is definitely not a UAV."

A voice Tony recognized as Major Allen came over the speaker. "What is it, then?" Allen asked.

"I think it's a . . . it's a man, sir."

"Whiplash Two," Viper One said, "it's still there. Roll! Roll!"

Tony clung tight as the airplane began a series of dizzying rolls, twists, and spins—up, down, sideways, and back again. Inside his armor, Tony began to feel queasy.

"Sir," Jarvis's calm voice said, "in two minutes, we won't have sufficient power to return home."

Iron Man lost his grip and tumbled through the air. He smashed into Whiplash Two's left wing, ripping it off. The jet careened toward the ground.

"I'm hit!" Whiplash Two cried. He pushed the eject button and the canopy of his aircraft flew off. The rocket-powered cockpit chair zoomed clear of the crippled aircraft, but the chair's parachute failed to open.

"Whiplash One," Major Allen called, "do you see a chute?"

"Negative!" Whiplash One replied. "No chute! No chute!"

Iron Man streaked forward, angling for the falling pilot.

"Power critical," Jarvis intoned. "Set course for home immediately."

"The UAV is going after him!" Whiplash One cried. "It's attacking!"

The heads-up display gave Tony the information he needed. He rocketed toward the falling pilot. At the last instant, Iron Man's metal fingers found the jammed chute mechanism and ripped it open.

The pilot's chute deployed with a loud whooshing sound. The parachute caught the air and jerked the pilot upward, away from Iron Man. The chute billowed out, gliding the pilot safely toward earth.

Beneath his helmet, Tony grinned.

"Good chute! Good chute!" Whiplash One called. "You're not going to believe this, but that UAV just saved his life!"

Iron Man fired his thrusters, banking sharply, and barely avoided slamming into the ground. Whiplash One executed a barrel roll and came up right on his tail.

Nearly every system in Tony's armor was flashing

CRITICAL. He didn't have the power for any more fancy maneuvers; he barely had the power to make it back home.

Then the jet peeled off his tail and roared away. Tony realized Rhodey was still on the phone. "Tony, you still there?"

"Hey, thanks," Tony said.

"You owe me a plane. You know that, right?"

"Well," Tony said, "technically he hit me. Now are you going to come by and see what I'm working on?"

"No, no, no," Rhodey said. "The less I know, the better. Now what am I supposed to tell the press?"

"Training exercise," Tony said. "Isn't that the usual?"

"It's not that simple," Rhodey said.

CHAPTER 15

Pepper sat on a small couch in the living room, her head propped in her hands. There had been no sign of Tony in almost a full day. Hours ago, she had decided to wait up for his return. But she was dozing now, exhausted from the strain of wondering where Tony was. She woke up as she heard a familiar voice on TV: It was Rhodey giving a press conference about the training exercise in which an F-22 had crashed the day before.

A sudden whooshing sound startled her awake. The house shook, as though something very heavy had fallen over downstairs in the lab. She went down and heard

Tony's voice while she was still on the stairs. "Hey!" he said. "I designed this to come off, so . . ."

He saw her as she came into the lab. "Hey," he said, like nothing was unusual. But he was in what looked like a red-and-gold suit of armor, with Jarvis running a thicket of robot arms trying to take pieces of it off his body. "Please try not to move, sir," Jarvis said.

"What's going on here?" Pepper asked. She had seen Tony design a lot of crazy things, but never anything like this. It looked brutal, all armored strength.

"Let's face it," he said. "This is not the worst thing you've caught me doing."

But she was in no mood to joke. "Are those . . . bullet holes?" she asked.

Tony tried to think of the best way to tell her the truth.

A train of black SUVs wound through the desert toward Raza's hideout. The vehicles stopped near the warlord's tent, and private security guards stepped out. They took up defensive positions around the convoy.

Obadiah Stane stepped from his SUV as warlord Raza pulled back the tent flaps.

"Welcome," Raza said. Seeing Stane's gaze linger on his scarred face, he added, "Compliments of Tony Stark."

"If you'd killed him when you were supposed to," Stane said, "you'd still have a face."

Raza's smile turned into a savage grimace. "You paid us trinkets to kill a prince," the warlord said. "An insult, both to me and to the lord whose ring I wear." He held up his hand, showing the symbol of Ten Rings, interlocked, on the one ring he wore.

"I think it is best we don't get your master involved in this," Stane said. "I've come a long way to see this weapon. Show me."

Raza nodded. "Come. Leave your guards outside."

Stane entered the tent and stared. The weapon was gray, human-sized, and hanging from wires near the rear of the yurt. It resembled a high-tech suit of medieval armor. It was scarred and pitted, nearly destroyed before being pieced back together.

"Stark's escape bore unexpected fruit," Raza said.

Stane nodded slowly. "So this is how he did it."

"This is only a crude first effort," Raza said. "From what my men tell me of their recent battle, I believe Stark has perfected the design."

He handed Stane a set of grainy surveillance photos showing a man in red-and-gold armor wreaking havoc in Gulmira. Two of Raza's men brought in a battered laptop and reams of yellowed paper filled with drawings and schematics.

"What's this?" Stane asked.

"The inside of Tony Stark's mind," Raza replied. He shuffled the papers around until they fit together like a giant jigsaw puzzle. The puzzle revealed the form of Iron Man.

"These contain everything you will need to build this weapon," Raza said as Stane studied the plans. "Stark has made a masterpiece of death. A man with a dozen of these could rule from the Pacific to the Ukraine. You dream of Stark's throne, Mr. Stane. It seems we have a common enemy."

Stane ran his fingers over the armor, putting his hand through the hole in the chest plate.

"If we are back in business," Raza said, "I give you these designs as my gift. In turn, I hope you will repay me with the gift of iron soldiers."

Stane smiled and put his hands on Raza's shoulders.

"Take this gift as advance payment," Stane said. A sharp whine sounded close to the back of Raza's head.

For a moment, Raza looked puzzled. Then he collapsed to the ground, a victim of Stane's hidden sonic Taser. Stane removed the earplugs that had protected him from the device's effects.

"Technology. It's always been your Achilles' heel in this part of the world," Stane said. He showed Raza the tiny Taser, barely the size of a thumb drive. "Don't worry. It'll only last for fifteen minutes. That's the least of your problems."

He glanced at the ring on Raza's hand. "It'll be pretty hard for you to explain this to your master."

Stane turned and exited the tent. As expected, his men had easily rounded up Raza's troops. The warlord's men knelt, bound and gagged, near the SUVs.

"Crate up the armor and the rest of it," Stane told his lead guard. "All right. Let's finish up here."

Gunfire sounded as he walked back to the lead SUV.

Tony was working on final repairs and a few upgrades to the suit when Pepper came in. "Hey," he said. "You busy? Mind if I send you on an errand? I need you to go to my office."

He took a finger-sized USB drive from his worktable and handed it to Pepper.

"You're going to hack into the Stark Industries mainframe and retrieve all the recent shipping manifests. They're probably under 'Executive Files.' If not, they put it on a ghost drive, in which case you need to look for the lowest numeric heading."

"And what do you plan to do with this information if I bring it back here?" Pepper replied.

"Same drill," Tony said. "They've been dealing weapons under the table, and I'm going to stop them. I'm going to find my weapons and destroy them."

"Tony, you know I would help you with anything," she said. "But I cannot help you if you're going to start this again," she said.

"There is nothing except this," Tony said. "There's no art opening, no benefit, no business decision to be made. There's the next mission and nothing else."

"Is that so?" Pepper said. She paused. Then she set the USB drive on the table and said, "I quit."

Tony arched an eyebrow at her. "Really? You stood by my side when all I did was reap the benefits of wholesale destruction, and now that I'm trying to protect the people I put in harm's way, you're going to walk out?"

"You're going to kill yourself, Tony," she said. "I'm not going to be a part of it."

"I'm not crazy, Pepper," Tony said. He couldn't lose her. More than even she knew, he depended on her. "I just finally know what I have to do...and I know in my heart that it's right."

She looked at him for a long time. Then, like she was reading his mind, she said, "You're all I have, too, you know."

CHAPTER 16

Pepper hurried through the darkened halls of Stark Industries. She knew the corridors like the back of her hand. But sneaking around for Tony made her nervous.

Fortunately, she hadn't run into anyone on her way to Tony's office. She turned on his computer and plugged in the device he'd given her.

The gadget quickly began hacking into all the computers in the network. It took a moment, but it located the ghost drive and Pepper spawned a window full of folders.

As she opened each, she got more and more surprised and angry.

Orders for Jericho missiles, shipping manifests, schematics, and blueprints flashed on the screen.

"What are you up to, Obadiah?" she asked quietly.

An icon for a video file appeared on-screen. She clicked it open and watched as the image sprang to life.

The picture showed Tony, very beaten up, tied to a chair in a cave. Thuggish-looking guards surrounded him. One of the guards spoke.

"You did not tell us that the target you paid us to kill was the great Tony Stark," the brutish man said. "As you can see, Obadiah Stane, your deception and lies will cost you dearly. The price to kill Tony Stark has just gone up."

Pepper's jaw dropped. Just then, the office door opened, and Stane walked in.

"So, what are we going to do about this?" he asked.

Pepper tried to look Stane in the eye, but she was also watching the progress of the download as the USB drive copied all of Stane's files—including the hostage video. She nodded at Stane and tried to smile.

"I was so happy when he came home," Stane said. "It

was like we got him back from the dead. Now I realize...
well, Tony never really did come home, did he? Breaks
my heart."

"Well, he's a complicated person," Pepper said. Stane
started to come around the desk to greet her and at that
moment the download finished. She was just able to click
back to the home screen and cover the USB drive with a
newspaper before Stane got close enough to see what she
was doing.

"He's been through a lot," she went on. "I think he'll
be all right."

"You are a very rare woman," Stane said. "Tony doesn't
know how lucky he is."

"Thank you," Pepper said. As smoothly as she could,
she swept up the newspaper and in the same motion
pinched the USB drive out of the computer. "I'd better get
back there."

Stane walked her to the office door. "Is that today's
paper?" he asked as she was walking out.

She stopped, suddenly terrified that he was onto her,
that he would try to do something to her. "Yes," she said.
All she could do was try to play it cool.

Stane came over to her and extended a hand. "Do you
mind?"

"Not at all," she said, handing it to him.

He grinned. "Puzzle."

"Of course," she said.

"Take care," Obadiah said.

Pepper walked down the hallway feeling like she had a huge bull's-eye on her back. In the elevator, she kept waiting for an alarm to go off...but she got to the lobby and was walking across it when she saw Agent Coulson of S.H.I.E.L.D. at the security desk.

"Ms. Potts," Coulson said, "did you forget our appointment?"

"Nope," Pepper replied, latching onto his arm. "Of course not. Right now. Come with me." She took his arm and started walking faster.

"Right now?"

"Yeah, walk with me," she said. "I'm going to give you the meeting of your life. Your office."

As soon as they were out the door, she felt like she could breathe again. At least for now.

In a subbasement of Stark Industries, Obadiah Stane spoke to a group of the company's best engineers. Before them sat Iron Man's old gray armor, disassembled into its component pieces.

As the engineers worked to replicate the armor's parts, Stane walked among them, supervising.

The head engineer took him aside. "Mr. Stane. Sir, we've explored what you've asked of us and it seems as though there's a little hiccup. Actually, um . . . "

"A hiccup?"

The engineer nodded. "Yes, see, to power the suit . . . sir, the technology doesn't actually exist. So it—"

"Wait, wait, the technology?" Stane repeated. He pointed at the Arc Reactor, looming over them. "William, William . . . here is the technology! I've asked you to simply make it smaller."

"Yes, sir." The engineer nodded. "That's what we're trying to do, but . . . honestly, it's impossible—"

Stane glared at him. "Tony Stark was able to build this in a cave. With a box of scraps!"

"Well," the engineer said, "I'm not Tony Stark."

Tony finished getting the suit back up to speed and went upstairs, figuring a shower and something to eat would be next on the agenda. His phone chirped and he noted Pepper's number on the caller ID. He answered the phone and started to greet her when sudden paralyzing pain shot through his entire body.

Tony slumped on his couch as Obadiah Stane came into his field of vision and showed him a device Tony recognized as a sonic Taser.

He heard Pepper's voice coming from his phone. "Tony? Tony, are you there?"

"Breathe," Stane said with a wicked smile. He hung up on Pepper and removed the earplugs that baffled the Taser's signal. "Easy, easy. You remember this one, right? Shame the government didn't approve it. There're so many applications for causing short-term paralysis."

He set a briefcase down on the couch, opened it, and took a knife out to cut a hole in Tony's shirt, exposing the mini Arc Reactor. "When I ordered the hit on you," Stane said conversationally, "I worried I was killing the golden goose. But, you see, it was fate that you survived that."

Tony tried to move, but all he could do was track Stane with his eyes. He could hear, he could see, but he couldn't move his arms or his legs. Stane used the knife to loosen up the Arc Reactor in its housing. "Do you really think that just because you have an idea, it belongs to you? Your father, he helped give us the atomic bomb. What kind of world would it be today if he was as selfish as you?"

Stane twisted the Arc Reactor and loosened it from the housing. Then with a snap, he pulled it out of Tony's chest.

Tony felt his heart slow down and begin to stop.

"Ohh, isn't it beautiful," Stane said. "Tony, this is your Ninth Symphony. This is your legacy. A new generation of weapons with this at its heart. Weapons that will help put the balance of power in our hands. The right hands."

He stood up and put the Arc Reactor in the briefcase. Then he snapped it shut and looked down at Tony, who was struggling to breathe. "I wish you could have seen my prototype," Stane said. "It's not as … well, not as conservative as yours. Oh, and it's too bad you had to involve Pepper in this."

Stane turned then, and without another word, he walked out of Tony's house, switching off the lights on his way.

CHAPTER 17

W hat do you mean he paid to have Tony killed?"
Rhodey blared. "Why should Obadiah...? Where
is Tony now?"

Pepper tried to keep her voice calm. "I don't know,"
she said into the receiver. "He's not answering his phone,
and Jarvis didn't pick up, either. Will you go to the mansion and check on him? I'm going to look in the labs
here."

"Is that safe?" Rhodey asked.

"I've got some government men with me," Pepper
replied. "I think we can handle it."

"If Tony's at the mansion, I'll find him," Rhodey assured her.

"Thanks, Rhodey." She signed off, glad that Agent Coulson had brought five other agents with him. They'd need a small army to go against Stane and the resources of Stark Industries.

Her first priority, though—now that she'd convinced Coulson to help her—had to be finding Tony. If he was on campus, the high-tech lab below the Arc Reactor would be the place to start looking. Unfortunately, Stane would know that, too.

A chill ran down Pepper's spine as they headed for the lab. She prayed that she and Rhodey weren't already too late.

Obadiah Stane stepped into the subbasement lab of Stark Industries, below the Arc Reactor. In his hand, he held the glowing RT heart he'd stolen. The overhead lights were off; everyone had gone home. Only the dim red security lights lit his way as he walked purposefully across the room.

The prototype armor—the armor that would make Stark's shareholders even richer—stood in a corner, next to the Sampson cluster machines that had manufactured it and the original armor.

Carefully, Stane opened the new armor's chest plate and locked the stolen heart into place.

The sensors in the faceplate of the helmet glowed to life—twin eyes, burning red in the darkness.

Stane smiled.

Tony gasped for breath as the elevator doors slid open, revealing his workshop. He tried to take a step, but his knees buckled and he fell on his face.

Slowly, painfully, he began crawling across the workshop floor. He could see his goal—encased in shatterproof plastic—sitting on the table on the far side of the lab: his old chest piece. Thank heaven Pepper had saved it.

It was less than fifty feet away, but it seemed like miles. Tony's heart pounded. At any moment, the shrapnel might kill him.

He reached the bench and hoisted himself up, fumbling

for the plastic container. His hand brushed against it, but he didn't have the strength to move it. He collapsed to the floor and lay there, thinking that it was really going to happen. He was really going to die. And so was Pepper.

Then the case fell to the floor next to him.

He looked up and there was Dummy beeping and whirring. Tony said something he never thought he'd say to Dummy: "Good boy."

With the last of his strength, he smashed the case and got the old RT in his hand.

Maybe, thanks to the dumbest robot in the lab, he wasn't quite dead yet after all.

Agent Coulson placed something on the hinges of the locked door leading to the subbasement lab. Pepper's pass code wasn't working for some reason, and none of them wanted to waste time trying to figure out why. "Oh, what's that?" she asked. "Like, a thing that's going to pick the lock?"

"You might want to take a few steps back," Coulson said, and did exactly that himself.

Everyone retreated around the corner of the stairwell

and crouched down. Coulson pressed a button and the door blew off its hinges. Pepper thought, not for the first time, that maybe she was in the wrong line of work.

Agent Coulson led the group through the smoking doorway and into the corridor beyond. Pepper noticed the security camera staring down at them from one corner of the ceiling. If Tony was here, would he be watching them? Would Stane?

The huge laboratory ahead was dark, lit only by the blinking lights of the automated machinery, which filled the room almost to overflowing. It had been a long time since Pepper had been down here, and everything looked different—sinister.

"Tony?" she called tentatively. "Obadiah?"

Something moved in the darkness. Pepper jumped. All the agents drew their guns and swung around. Coulson shone a flashlight in that direction.

But it was only a battered suit of armor—apparently the one Tony had used to escape his kidnappers.

"What's that?" Coulson asked.

"New project," Pepper replied. "You shouldn't even be seeing it."

"Looks pretty old to me," another of the agents commented.

"I wasn't talking about the armor," Coulson said, "I was talking about the empty hooks next to it."

Pepper looked at the hooks, perplexed. Just at that moment, something grabbed one of the agents at the rear of the group and yanked him into the darkness.

Rhodey reeled back and kicked the front door of Tony's mansion off its hinges. Inside, the home was eerily dark and silent; Jarvis didn't greet Rhodey as he entered.

The living room was in shambles. Furniture lay overturned, several lamps had been broken. An untouched, deep-dish pizza lay on the coffee table.

"Tony?" Rhodey called. "Jarvis?"

There was no answer.

"Tony, where are you?"

Rhodey went to the elevator leading to the lab, but it seemed to be locked on the lower floor. He found the stairway and jumped down the steps three at a time. The door to the lab was locked, too, so he kicked it open.

His jaw dropped as he stepped inside. The entire workshop seemed to have been turned into an armory.

Electronic components lay everywhere. Rows of helmets, boots, and gauntlets filled the laboratory shelves. Two suits of gleaming armor hung in the middle of the room, suspended by cables that were attached to the ceiling. They looked like the surveillance photos Rhodey had seen of the UAV that attacked the Gulmiran rebels.

"Tony?" he called again.

Tony Stark lay on the floor, looking like eight miles of bad road. But he was alive. Robotic arms moved around him in an intricate dance, performing surgery on Tony's chest plate.

"Tony, you okay?" Rhodey asked.

Tony gazed darkly at him. "Where's Pepper?"

"She's fine. She's with five agents. They're about to arrest Obadiah."

The robot arms finished their task and retracted into the ceiling. "That's not going to be enough," Tony said, standing. He took down the red-and-gold armor and began putting it on.

"What's the plan?" Rhodey asked.

"I'm going after Stane," Tony replied. He finished donning the armor and lowered the helmet over his head.

"That's the coolest thing I've ever seen," Rhodey said.

Tony almost cracked a smile, but he was all business. Rhodey understood why. He'd been almost killed twice by his friend and mentor, and now his...well, Pepper wasn't his girlfriend. But she meant everything to him, and she was in danger.

"Not bad, huh?" Tony said. "Let's do it."

Rhodey nodded. "You need me to do anything else?"

Tony nodded back and said, "Keep the skies clear." With a sound like a jet engine taking off, his boot rockets fired and he soared out through a ragged hole in the workshop roof.

Rhodey watched for a moment, in awe. Then he remembered the other suit of armor—the silver one. He pulled the helmet off the rack, and admired it.

"Next time, baby," Rhodey said. He raced to the garage on the far side of the lab, picked out the fastest car he could find, and zoomed off, chasing his friend.

Pepper dodged through the lab equipment, trying to keep out of sight. Something terrible had happened, but she couldn't be sure what. From behind the empty hooks, a set of lights had come on...like eyes, and an Arc Reactor.

Like a much larger version of Tony's armor. Then it burst out into the huge armory space. They had all been on the run since.

Gunfire sounded from somewhere nearby. Bullets burst pipes, spewing steam into the semidarkness. Pepper moved in the opposite direction, trying to put as much machinery between her and the gunfire as possible.

She plugged her cell phone into her ear and tried to get a signal. Nothing.

Something exploded, and a big piece of metal zipped past. It smashed through several pipes, sending more steam into the air.

An agent stumbled out of the mist toward her. "Agents down! Agents down!" he called into his radio. Spotting Pepper, he added, "Get out of here!"

He pushed her toward the exit, which she could barely make out through the smoke. She ran for it.

Behind her, the lab entryway shattered into a spray of dust and debris, but Pepper didn't dare look back. She ran up the stairway, slowing to catch her breath only when she reached the third landing.

The wall below her shook as something smashed through the door. But the thing was too big for the stairwell; it got stuck in the debris. It was a huge metal suit of armor—much bigger than the one she'd seen hanging in the lab or the one Tony used. It looked like a cross between a man and a tank. Its red eyes glowed in the semidarkness.

Pepper turned and ran as fast as she could. She didn't look back.

When she got outside, she punched Tony's number on her cell phone. Much to her relief, he answered immediately.

"Tony, thank goodness I got you!" she said. "Listen to me—"

"Pepper," Tony replied, "where are you?"

Suddenly, the ground beneath her shook. She toppled sideways, and her earpiece fell from her head. An armored fist blasted through the pavement at her feet. Another fist punched through, widening the hole. The hands peeled the asphalt back like a flimsy candy wrapper.

The armored form of Iron Monger burst up through the crater. It was the first time she'd gotten a look at the whole suit, and it was terrifying. It stood maybe fifteen feet high, maybe twenty, and it was as wide as four or five men. Missiles bristled from launchers on its shoulders and arms. Pepper backed away, stumbling over the broken pavement. The iron giant towered over her.

"Look..." Pepper said, backing away.

Iron Monger stepped forward, pieces of asphalt and rebar showering down around him. "Where do you think you're going?" his amplified voice growled through distorting speakers. "Your services are no longer required."

CHAPTER 18

Pepper threw herself flat on the ground as Iron Man zoomed over her head, activating the repulsors in both hands. The blasts hit Iron Monger, and he staggered backward. Iron Man kept coming, smashing his fists into the giant's armored chest. "For thirty years, I've been propping you up!" Stane roared. "I built this company from nothing and nothing is going to stand in my way! Least of all you!"

Iron Monger was bigger, heavier, and much stronger. Tony had to get away and use his quickness or he wasn't going to live very long.

Iron Monger swiped at Iron Man and grabbed hold of Tony's outstretched gauntlet. Both of them tumbled into the crater Iron Monger had ripped in the pavement.

They smashed through a cement wall and then through the retaining wall that separated the Stark Industries buildings from the nearby highway.

Drivers slammed on their brakes and cars careened out of control as the metal titans crashed down in the middle of the road. An experimental hydrogen-powered bus skidded and slammed into the retaining wall. As Iron Man and Iron Monger stepped apart, the bus's passengers ran for safety.

Iron Monger grabbed a station wagon and hefted it over his head. The family inside the car screamed.

"Don't," Tony told him. "This is our fight."

"Collateral damage, Tony," Iron Monger replied. "It's part of the game."

Tony hit his repulsors, but nothing happened; probably they'd been damaged in the fight.

"Divert power to chest RT!" Tony said.

"Power reduced to nineteen percent," Jarvis said.

"Now!"

Energy surged through the RT in Iron Man's chest plate. A powerful repulsor burst blasted forth and struck Iron Monger full in the chest, making him stagger. As the giant fell, he heaved the car toward Tony.

Iron Man caught the vehicle, but the weight forced him to his knees. The armor's servos whirred, but their power had been drained by the massive repulsor blast. Tony's old RT heart didn't have the energy of the new one Stane had stolen.

Iron Man's armor buckled and the station wagon fell on top of him. Iron Monger recovered and thundered toward his victims once more.

"Go, Mom! Go!" a kid in the station wagon cried. The woman inside stomped on the gas and the car took off, dragging Iron Man with it. Sparks flew as Tony's armor scraped across the pavement.

Iron Monger followed, stepping on some cars, batting others out of the way. Drivers that were caught on the roadway stopped and fled from their vehicles.

Tony finally managed to pull himself out from under the station wagon. He staggered to his feet, his armor smoking. Iron Monger grabbed the front wheel of an abandoned motorcycle and smashed the bike into Iron Man.

Pepper's voice came over the headset. "Tony," she said, "this is not looking good."

Iron Man sailed through the air for a hundred yards and smashed into the retaining wall right next to the hydrogen-powered bus. Iron Monger blasted off, his immense bulk hurtling forward like a cannonball.

Tony tried his hand repulsors again; still no luck. "Jarvis!" he said.

"Working on resolving the problem, sir."

Iron Monger landed on top of Iron Man and pressed one huge boot into his chest.

Tony grunted with the impact and tried to lift the boot off. But saving the station wagon had depleted even more of his power reserves.

Slowly, Iron Monger applied pressure to his boot, crushing Iron Man into the ground.

CHAPTER 19

Iron Man felt his armor buckling. Iron Monger towered above him, easily twice his size and three times his weight. A roaring sound filled Tony's ears. At first, he thought it was the rushing of his own blood.

Then twin headlights blazed in the darkness as a sports car sped right toward them. Iron Monger spotted the car and turned—too late. The car smashed into the giant's other leg. The leg's armor buckled and Iron Monger careened through the air, his jet boots crippled.

He crashed into a parked bus, bursting its hydrogen

tank. Iron Monger struggled to free himself from the wreckage, but his metal fingers set off a spark and... WHOOM!

The whole bus went up in a huge fireball.

Tony staggered to his feet. The sports car that had saved him was crushed and mangled, but he still recognized it—and the driver inside.

"Rhodey!" he called, ripping the wreck open so his friend could climb out.

Rhodey grinned at him.

"Did you have to use my car?" Tony asked.

Rhodey shrugged. "It's not like you don't have more."

The two of them stared at the bus, now just a mass of flames and molten metal.

"Get this area evacuated," Tony said. "The Arc Reactor is about to melt down." As he spoke, Jarvis finished rerouting his armor's power reserves. Iron Man activated his boots and jetted into the air.

"Impressive! You've upgraded your armor!" Stane shouted up into the sky.

Then rockets fired in Iron Monger's massive boots, and it, too, rose into the sky. "I've made some upgrades of my own!" Stane added.

"Sir," Jarvis said, "it appears his suit can fly."

"Duly noted," Tony said. "Take me to maximum altitude."

"With fifteen percent power," Jarvis protested mildly, "the odds of reaching—"

"I know the math!" Tony shouted. "Do it!"

He rocketed higher, with Iron Monger close on his tail. "Thirteen percent power, sir," Jarvis said. "Eleven percent...seven percent..."

"Just leave it on the screen," Tony snapped. "Stop telling me!"

Iron Monger was close to catching him. "You had a great idea, Tony," Stane shouted over the collective blast of their rockets, "but my suit is more advanced in every way!"

"How'd you solve the icing problem?" Tony asked.

"Icing problem?"

Stane hadn't been paying attention. He'd been too focused on catching Tony. But now ice had built up in such thick chunks over the Iron Monger suit's controls that abruptly its rockets cut out.

"Might want to look into it," Tony said as Iron Monger began the long fall back to earth.

"We are now running on emergency backup power," Jarvis noted. Tony dove back toward earth, hoping he wouldn't end up in free fall, too.

Iron Monger crashed into the top of the Stark complex and through several levels of service tunnels into the sub-basement lab. Tony followed, splashing down amid a lake of water and cooling fluid from ruptured pipes. For a moment, steam and debris obscured everything.

As Tony struggled to his feet, the whole building shuddered. Warning lights flashed and a Klaxon horn sounded. The heads-up display in Iron Man's armor relayed a message from the Stark Industries computer systems: ARC REACTOR HOUSING CRACKED. MELTDOWN IMMINENT.

Iron Man walked through the rubble of the lab, but he didn't see Iron Monger—or, for that matter, Obadiah Stane—anywhere. Tony set his systems to scan for his enemy.

"Pepper..." he called over his communications link.

"Tony!" she called back. "Are you okay?"

"I'm almost out of power," he said. "I've got to get out of this thing. I'll be right there."

He started to lift off out of the crash site, but Iron Monger caught him. "Nice try!" Stane laughed.

"Weapons status?" Tony inquired of Jarvis.

"Repulsors off-line. Missiles off-line?"

That left... "Flares!" Tony shouted.

The flares went off in Iron Monger's face, blinding Stane, who reflexively let go. Tony had a new idea, but each of his new ideas was getting more desperate. He wouldn't have too many more chances.

"Pepper?"

"Tony!"

"This isn't working. We're going to have to overload the reactor and blast the roof."

"How are you going to do that?" She sounded worried.

"You're going to do that," Tony replied.

"Me?"

"Yes. I want you to go to the central console and open up all the circuits. When I get clear of the roof, I'll let you know. You're going to hit the master bypass button."

"Okay, I'm going in," she said.

Tony kept scanning for Iron Monger, but the steam, debris, and water were fouling up his imaging systems. He headed for the roof on the last dregs of his power. Pretty soon, the suit would be no more protective than a medieval knight's plate.

He found the cable he would need to complete the feed-back circuit and channel the reactor overload. "Pepper," he said, "I'm about to complete the circuit. Once I do, it's going to discharge all of the reactor's power and channel it up through the roof. Get ready to push the emergency master bypass—"

"I've found it!" she called.

"—but not until I'm off the roof," he finished. "It's going to fry everything up here."

He detached his left gauntlet, leaving the cable clamped in place. The screen on his heads-up display flashed: CIRCUIT COMPLETE.

Tony flipped up his faceplate and wiped the sweat from his eyes. "Pepper," he said, "wait until I fly clear, and then hit the button."

The roof shuddered, and Tony wheeled as Iron Monger landed twenty feet away. Flames still licked around Iron Monger's blackened armor as he lumbered toward Iron Man.

Tony barely managed to get his faceplate down before Iron Monger struck. The giant's huge armored fist smashed into Iron Man's chest.

Iron Man skidded back across the rooftop and tumbled to his feet. He blasted off, flying straight for his enemy. Schematics of Iron Monger armor appeared on Tony's heads-up display, showing the probable location of the giant's hydraulic control systems.

Iron Man reached for the controls with his remaining

gauntlet, but Iron Monger spun and caught him in a massive bear hug. Tony gasped as his armor began to crack under the pressure. Inside his helmet, the heads-up display crystals splintered and went dark.

"Jarvis," Tony gasped. "Deploy countermeasures!"

Instantly compartments on the armor flipped open and a thousand particles of chaff exploded, filling the air with smoke, flame, and bits of metal.

Surprised, Iron Monger lost his grip and Tony rocketed free. He landed behind his foe and ripped Iron Monger's hydraulics loose. "You ripped out my targeting system!" Stane shouted.

Iron Monger staggered, and Iron Man punched him. The giant fell back, flailing desperately. His metal fingers latched onto Iron Man's helmet. He whirled, tossing Iron Man like a doll.

Iron Man bounced to a halt atop the bank of skylights above the Arc Reactor core. Tony gasped as the evening breeze ruffled his hair. Iron Monger had ripped off his helmet!

The giant laughed as he crushed the depowered helmet like a tin can.

Iron Man staggered to his feet, standing atop the skylights. He and Iron Monger faced each other. Iron Monger lumbered forward, and Tony realized, for the first time, that the giant's armor had built-in machine guns.

Tony jumped aside as Iron Monger sprayed the roof with bullets. The huge glass skylights shattered beneath Iron Man, but without his helmet controls, he couldn't fire his jets.

He caught on to the side of the roof at the last instant. He heard a gasp below him and, glancing down, saw Pepper standing near the reactor core. As Tony pulled himself back onto the roof, Iron Monger kept shooting.

Iron Man's armor stopped a few glancing blows, but Tony knew that without his helmet, sooner or later his luck would run out.

"How ironic, Tony! Trying to rid the world of weapons, you gave it its best one ever!" Iron Monger cried out. Stane had really gone around the bend, Tony thought.

"Pepper!" he shouted down through the skylights. "Hit the button!"

"You said not to!" she shouted back.

"Just do it!" Tony cried as another bullet dented his armor.

"But you'll die!"

"Pepper, we have no choice! We have to stop him! Do it now!"

CHAPTER 20

Pepper hit the button and dived for cover under the nearby consoles.

A pulse of electromagnetic energy flashed upward along the reactor housing and through the cable Tony had rigged up. The energy arced across the satellite dishes, vaporizing the roof between them.

The pulse spread outward, killing the power of everything it touched. The lab went dark, then the building, then the rest of the Stark Industries compound. And, on the roof of the Arc Reactor, the power to both suits of armor died as well.

Iron Monger and Iron Man stopped dead in their tracks, frozen like statues.

More energy burst forth. The roof shuddered and began to buckle and sag. Tony glanced down at his chest. His RT heart was dark and cold. He knew he didn't have much time.

Iron Monger's armor, which was closest to the section of roof that had been vaporized, toppled over. Only by luck did its depowered fingers catch the edge of the roof as it slid down the slope.

Tony's heart pounded in his chest. Sweat poured down his head. Using every bit of strength he possessed, he forced his armor to move, reaching out to save his enemy.

"Take my hand!" he called to Iron Monger.

But Tony suddenly realized that his foe wasn't trying to escape from the crippled giant's armor; he was trying to manually winch open his rocket launcher.

But doing so loosened Iron Monger's grip on the sagging roof. With a sudden jolt, the giant began to slide again.

"Noooo...!" Iron Monger called as he plunged over the ledge and into the reactor core. A pillar of energy rose into the sky, dissipating into the clouds. With a roof-shaking hiss, the white-hot plasma swallowed him and Iron Monger vanished forever.

Tony shook his head. Now he would never understand why Stane had done what he did. Just out of greed? It didn't seem worth it. He closed his eyes and waited on the roof, trying to steady himself. But with Iron Monger gone, the roof didn't sag any further. Ten minutes later, a pair of flashlights played across the surface of Iron Man's lifeless armor.

Tony opened his eyes and saw Rhodey and Pepper running toward him.

They pulled him away from the precipice and off the roof. Eventually, Jarvis—whose mainframe had been far enough away to avoid the electromagnetic pulse— managed to restore the armor's power.

Tony looked at the RT heart in his chest. It glowed faintly. Tony breathed a sigh of relief. He'd had a very close call, but Iron Man would live to fight another day.

The next day, Tony and Pepper walked along the hall-way of Stark Industries. All the destruction had drawn enough attention that everyone wasn't just going to ignore it. So, against his will, Tony agreed to do a press conference. Pepper, who was carrying a stack of newspapers and documents, shoved a typewritten paper into his hands.

He scooped up a newspaper from the stack she was carrying and read the headline: WHO IS IRON MAN?

Tony shook his head. Already the battle seemed like a half-remembered dream. His people had never found the Iron Monger armor; apparently, the Arc Reactor had vaporized it, and Stane with it.

"Iron Man..." Tony mused. "That's kind of catchy. I mean, it's not technically accurate, since the suit's a gold-titanium alloy... But it's kind of evocative. 'Iron Man.'"

"Here's your alibi," Coulson said, handing Tony a document. "You were on your yacht, *Avalon*, during the whole incident. I've got port papers that put you there all night and sworn statements from fifty of your guests."

"Maybe we should say it was just Pepper and me alone on the island," Tony suggested. "On the yacht, I mean."

Coulson pointed at the document. "That's what happened," he said. "Just read it, word for word."

Tony glanced over the document. "There's nothing about Stane here."

"That's being handled," Coulson said. "He's on

vacation, and small aircraft have such a poor safety record. This isn't my first rodeo, Mr. Stark."

"Thank you very much for all your help, Agent Coulson," Pepper said.

"That's what we do," Coulson said. "You'll be hearing from us."

"Let's get this show on the road," Tony said.

"You're not Iron Man," Pepper said.

"Am so," Tony said, just to be contrary.

She shrugged. "Suit yourself."

"You know, if I were Iron Man, I'd have this girlfriend who knew my true identity. She'd be a wreck, because she'd always be worrying that I was going to die, yet so proud of the man I'd become. She'd be wildly conflicted," he went on, stopping to face her before he had to go out for the press conference. "Which would only make her more crazy about me. Tell me you never think about that night."

"What night?" Pepper asked. She straightened his tie.

"You know."

"Are you talking about the night that we danced and went up on the roof, and then you went downstairs to get me a drink, and you left me there, by myself? Is that the night you're talking about?"

Tony tried to say something, but Pepper Potts was the

only person in the world who had ever been able to render him speechless.

"Will that be all, Mr. Stark?" she asked.

"Yes," Tony said. "That will be all, Ms. Potts."

Pepper entered the conference room ahead of Tony and introduced him to a room full of reporters from all over the country. Rhodey was also there, giving Tony his stern stick-to-the-script stare. "And now, Mr. Stark has prepared a statement," he said. "He will not be taking any questions. Thank you."

Tony stepped to the podium. "Been a while since I was in front of you," he said. "I figure I'll stick to the cards this time."

There were chuckles from the crowd.

"There's been speculation that I was involved in the events that occurred on the freeway and the rooftop," Tony began.

A reporter in the middle of the room cut him off. "I'm sorry, Mr. Stark, but do you honestly expect us to believe that was a bodyguard in a suit that conveniently appeared, despite the fact that you..."

"I know that it's confusing," Tony said. "But it's one thing to question the official story, and another thing entirely to make wild accusations, or insinuate that I'm a Super Hero."

The reporter shot back immediately. "I never said you were a Super Hero."

"You didn't? Well, good, because that would be outlandish and fantastic," Tony said. He was flailing and he knew it. "I'm just not the hero type. Clearly."

Rhodey leaned over to him. "Just stick to the cards, man."

Tony nodded. "Yeah." He looked at the cards, then back up at the waiting reporters and cameras.

Rhodey gave him the stare again.

Tony dropped the cards.

"The truth is...I am Iron Man," he said.

The room exploded into pandemonium.

CHAPTER 21

In a forgotten part of Russia, a flickering television screen showed Tony Stark's press conference on a loop. Ivan Vanko watched. He watched Tony Stark say "I am Iron Man." He had watched videos of Stark flying through the air. Fighting the enemies of America. The more he watched, alone except for the television and his cockatoo, Irina, the more he hated Tony Stark.

His father, Anton, had passed away just three days before. Since then Ivan had turned his small apartment into a workshop, because before Anton Vanko's death, he had told his son many things—and *shown* him many things. Ivan had learned the true stories of Anton's work and Tony Stark's crimes. He had absorbed as much of his father's knowledge as he could. He had sorted through old records and plans, notebooks and loose sheaves of paper covered in diagrams and equations.

Ivan shuffled through boxes and found a cardboard blueprint tube. On the peeling label he read the English words: STARK INDUSTRIES. Underneath were two names: HOWARD STARK and ANTON VANKO. Ivan returned to the worktable and spread out the blueprints in the spill of lamplight. It was time for him to claim his heritage...and for Tony Stark to learn the bitter truth about his own.

CHAPTER 22

Tony decided Iron Man was going to be a part of whatever he did from here on out. He'd revealed the truth and he didn't try to keep his Iron Man suit a secret. Anytime someone needed him to help keep the peace, he was there. Over the next six months, he rescued hostages, defused standoffs, and twice brought small countries back from the brink of war—all that in just the first six months after the big Iron Monger fight and press conference revealing he was Iron Man.

Then it was time to put Iron Man to a different kind of use: kicking off the Stark Expo. It was one of the world's biggest gatherings of geniuses and inventors, where they all got together to showcase their new ideas.

For the opening ceremony, the crowd poured into the Tent of Tomorrow. They had already been treated to a montage on the giant video screens of Iron Man's recent exploits: an aerial tango with a barrage of shoulder-fired missiles, a lightning raid on a pirate ship off the Horn of Africa, a head-on collision with an air-to-air missile whose explosion coming over the Expo sound system was loud enough to register on nearby seismometers. The crowd loved it. They loved it even more when the real Iron Man rocketed down and landed at the center of the stage.

Robot arms unlocked the invisible joints on the Mark IV suit and took it apart. From the crowd's perspective, it appeared that Iron Man had been disassembled and a tuxedo-clad Tony Stark constructed in his place. The whole procedure took only seconds.

"It's good to be back!" he called out. He paused for a moment to get his breath. Six months earlier, when he'd turned himself into the armored Super Hero, he hadn't known what a physical toll it would take. Between the explosions, the late nights, and some troubles with the Arc Reactor, Tony Stark was worn down. But he had a show to put on.

"Blow something up!" a guy called from the crowd.

"Blow something up?" Tony echoed. "I already did that. I'm not saying that the world is enjoying its longest period of uninterrupted peace in years because of me. I'm not saying that from the ashes of captivity, never has a greater Phoenix metaphor been personified in human history. I'm not saying that Uncle Sam can kick back on a lawn chair, sippin' on an iced tea, because I haven't come across anyone who's man enough to go toe to toe with me on my best day...Please...It's not about me. It's not about...you...It's not even about us; it's about legacy. It's about what we choose to leave behind for future generations and that's why, for the next year and for the first time since 1974, the best and brightest men and women of nations and corporations the world over will pool their resources, share their collective vision to leave behind a brighter future. It's not about us! Therefore what I am saying, if I'm saying anything, is welcome back to the Stark Expo! And now, making a special guest appearance from the great beyond, to tell you what it's all about. Please welcome my father, Howard."

Tony stepped offstage as Howard Stark appeared on the screen, shown in his workshop sometime around 1970.

"Everything is achievable through technology," Howard

Stark said in the old film footage. "Better living, robust health, and—for the first time in human history—the possibility of world peace!" He gave the camera a nervous smile as he walked to a scale model of that first Expo.

Applause from the crowd swelled as the lights cut out and the music picked up, booming through the darkness as the crowd went nuts all over again. The Stark Expo, bigger and better than ever, was under way.

CHAPTER 23

After his appearance, Tony signed a replica of an Iron Man mask for a little kid and scribbled a few other autographs on the way to the backstage doors. Tony was running out of gas—fast. He staggered from exhaustion. Happy held him up. Looking around to see if anyone had noticed Tony's stumble, Hap asked, "You okay, man?"

"Aces," Tony said, even though it wasn't true. He'd started to notice odd discolorations around the Arc Reactor housing in his chest. You couldn't see them right now because of his clothes, but tendrils of a sickly purple radiated out from it. He was pretty sure the palladium fuel cells powering the reactor were poisoning him. His blood toxicity was 18 percent on some scale Jarvis had come up with. It apparently ranged from Perfect to Dead, and he was too far from one and too close to the other.

Jarvis was trying to find a new power source for the reactor, but it was a race against time.

Happy shoved open the backstage door, and a fresh wave of shouts and flashes greeted them. Tony rose to the occasion, shrugging off Hap and playing to the crowd. Happy triggered the remote control that opened the roof of Tony's favorite set of wheels—a gray sports car. Tony grabbed the key from Happy. "I'm driving," he said.

As he approached the car, a woman leaning on it stood to meet him. "Pleased to meet you, Mr. Stark," she said.

Tony had no idea who she was. "You too, Ms....?"

"Marshal," she said. "As in US." She slapped an envelope onto his chest. "You are hereby ordered to appear before the Senate Armed Services Committee tomorrow at nine a.m.," she said. She let go of the envelope and turned away.

There was no way to get out of it, so the next day Tony was in Washington DC. It was not the first time Tony had testified before the Senate, but he had a feeling it was going to be the least pleasant. Why? Because the hearing was chaired by Senator Stern, who had never liked Tony and liked him even less now.

"Mr. Stark, according to these contracts, you agreed to provide the US taxpayers with"—Stern flipped through a file and read—"'all current and as yet undiscovered weapons systems.' Now, do you or do you not at present possess a very specialized weapon—"

"I do not."

"You do not," Stern repeated incredulously.

"It depends on how you define the word 'weapon,'" Tony said.

Stern became angry. "The Iron Man suit is the most powerful weapon on the face of the earth," he said. "Yet you use it to sell tickets to your theme park." The senator decided to try a new tactic. "I'd like to call upon Justin Hammer, our current primary defense contractor, as an expert witness."

Justin Hammer strode down the aisle to be sworn in, basking in the attention. He ran Hammer Industries, a huge rival company to Stark Industries. Since Tony had stopped making weapons, Hammer had stepped in to supply the US government. Tony and Hammer had never liked each other.

"Let the minutes reflect," Tony said into the microphone, "that I observe Mr. Hammer entering the chamber and am wondering if and when an expert will also be in attendance."

Senator Stern's gavel banged over an outburst of laughter. If Hammer was bothered, though, he didn't show it. "I may well not be an expert. But you know who was?" he asked, playing to the gallery but addressing the question to Tony. "Your dad. Howard Stark. A father to us all. And he knew that technology was the sword, not the shield, that protects this great nation."

Hammer went on. "Anthony Stark has created a sword with untold possibilities, and yet he insists it's a shield! He asks us to trust him as we cower behind it! I love peace, but we live in a world of grave threats."

Tony rolled his eyes. *Anthony?* Nobody had called him Anthony since maybe the first day of kindergarten, which he'd gone to only because other kids did.

"Thank you. God bless Iron Man, and God Bless America," Hammer said.

This gave Tony an idea. He slipped his new phone

out of his pocket. It was a rectangle of fiber optics, pure computing power that looked like a piece of clear plastic. He started fiddling with it while Senator Stern continued. "Thank you, Mr. Hammer. The committee would now like to invite Lieutenant Colonel James T. Rhodes into the chamber."

Tony looked toward the door, where Rhodey was entering in full dress uniform. He looked uncomfortable. Tony met him in the aisle and they shook hands. He was glad to see Rhodey there even though Rhodey didn't look happy to be there. If there was any living human Tony knew he could count on to do the right thing, that person was James Rhodes.

After Rhodey had been sworn in, Stern said, "I have before me a report on the Iron Man compiled by Lieutenant Colonel Rhodes. Colonel, please read into the minutes page fifty-seven, paragraph four."

"Certainly, Senator," Rhodey said. "May I first point out that I was not briefed on this hearing, nor prepared to testify—"

"Duly noted," Stern said without looking up from his notes. "Please continue."

Rhodey swallowed the snub and went on. "This paragraph out of context does not reflect the summary of my findings." Stern said nothing, and Rhodey had no choice but to read the indicated passage.

"'As he does not operate within any definable branch of government, Iron Man presents a potential threat to the security of both the nation and her interests.'" Rhodey looked up at the senators. "However, I went on to recommend that the benefits far outweigh the liabilities—"

"Colonel Rhodes," Stern interrupted. "Please read page fifty-six of your report."

Rhodey glanced at the indicated page and gestured to a bank of monitors, which lit up to display blurry satellite images. "Intelligence suggests that the devices seen in these photos are in fact all attempts at making manned copies of Mr. Stark's suit." With a laser pointer, he indicated points on each of the monitors where blurry images showed something like an armored suit.

Aha, Tony thought. He'd figured Stern would do this and now he had a chance to turn tables. He stood and touched an icon on his phone. "Let's see what's really going on here," he said as his phone took control of the monitor screens. "If . . . I . . . may," he began, as a series of classified videos loaded and began to play. At top left, a North Korean proving ground was hosting a test flight of a skeletal suit. Something like Tony's repulsors fired, lifting the suit and pilot into the air. "Wow, it looks like I have commandeered your screens," remarked Tony with a smile.

"And you're right," he continued. "North Korea is well on its..." Suddenly, the suit and pilot disappeared in a flash of light that overwhelmed the camera. When the image resolved, the smoking remains of the suit were being hosed down by firefighters. "Nope," Tony said. "Whew. That was a relief."

Similar results played out on the other monitors. "Let's see how Russia is doing....Oh, dear," Tony went on. "And Japan?...Oh, I guess not. India? Not so much. Germans are good engineers. Yowch. That's gonna leave a mark." Then he froze all the looping videos except one. He expanded that image until it took up the entire bank of monitors.

"Wait," Tony said. "The United States is in the game, too. Look, it's Justin Hammer." Glancing over his shoulder at the camera crews filming the hearing, Tony added, "You might want to push in on Hammer for this."

This last video showed Hammer, observing as a crew strapped someone into an armored exoskeleton. It was a bad imitation of the Iron Man suit. On the monitor, Hammer winked at the camera. The prototype suit lifted off and started a loop-the-loop that quickly turned into a crash when the thrusters cut out and pieces of the prototype started to fall off. The suit tumbled back to the ground, kicking up a huge plume of sand. Hammer could be heard yelling to cut the video.

In the Senate chamber, Hammer finally succeeded in unplugging the monitor. "Yeah, I'd say most countries are ten years away," Tony said. "Hammer Industries, maybe twenty."

Hammer looked like he had a mouthful of spoiled milk. "I would like to point out," he said, "that the test pilot survived and suffered only minor spinal bruising. He is currently white-water rafting with his family."

Tony turned to face the camera. "The good news is," Tony said, "I'm your nuclear deterrent. And it's working. We're safe. You're welcome. You want my property? You can't have it. I have successfully privatized world peace. What more do you want?"

Stern was shouting and pounding his gavel, but Tony ignored him. He hopped down from the lectern, flashed peace signs, and blew kisses. The cameras loved him.

CHAPTER 24

Fool, thought Ivan Vanko. He was working and watching Tony Stark's appearance on television.

Ivan's eyes watered and his neck ached from the fine soldering work required to build a functioning miniature Arc Reactor. Until that moment, only two had existed in the world. Now there was a third, tiny and perfect, glowing on his worktable. His father would have loved it. Ivan wanted to share the moment with someone, so he reached out toward Irina's perch and waited for her to climb onto his knuckles.

"Isn't it beautiful, Irina?"

She chirped her name back at him.

Ivan Vanko had made an Arc Reactor. He was the second man in history to do so. It would forever gall him that Stark was the first, that Stark had suppressed Anton Vanko's pioneering work and then taken sole credit for further developments. Ivan would have to console himself with being there when Tony Stark was destroyed.

Irina cackled. Outside, the sun was setting, and snow was beginning to fall. Ivan began to piece together the next part of his plan.

Ivan could have chosen any of a thousand different ways to destroy Stark, but in the end he chose the whip. His creation was five feet long, made of articulated tungsten carbide vertebrae. He had machined each vertebra himself and linked them together onto a woven cable. A handle, insulated and wired to the power supply, extended another six inches.

Ivan wound copper wire around the vertebrae, weaving it along the cable and through holes like the nerve openings in a spinal column. When the weapon was done and activated, Ivan would possess a whip of white-hot molten metal. Not even Stark's armor would survive it for long. Nothing could. Ivan finished wiring the whip. He shrugged into a harness he had built of leather-wrapped tungsten and placed the miniature Arc Reactor in a housing set over his sternum, mimicking the Iron Man chest plate.

He ran the cable from the glowing chest repulsor transmitter down his arm to the handle of the whip, attaching it at the shoulder, the bicep, and the radius. Before he plugged in the RT, Ivan put on a glove; even with the insulation, he wouldn't be able to hold the whip bare-handed. The glove extended well up his forearm and would protect him from accidental grazes of the whip.

When he plugged the power cable into the whip, it sparked to life with a hum that vibrated in Ivan's bones. He flicked it out to its full length, and bits of plasma jumped from the tip, searing holes where they landed. Irina squawked and fluttered her wings, scooting to the far end of her perch.

Now he needed to test it. The picture of Tony Stark on his television gave him the perfect target. Ivan flicked the whip away from his body and then pivoted to bring it down in a sweeping arc. The sight and sound of it connecting with the television was like a lightning strike with thunder. His ears rang, and his eyes watered from the flash. An involuntary grin spread across his face as he blinked away the tears and looked at what he had done.

The television lay split in two; the ancient screen and tube had exploded into sprays of glittering fragments. Ivan had not felt a thing, no sense of resistance or even impact. His grin broadened. He flipped the whip in a tight loop as if spinning a lasso, enjoying the sparks, then touched a stud on the inside of his wrist to turn it off.

One whip was good. Two would be even better.

Since Rhodey was stationed at Edwards Air Force Base, and since he and Tony had been friends for years, Pepper had reasoned that there were several good reasons for inviting Rhodey to ride with them back from Washington. It wasn't working out. She sat in a seat between her boss and her boss's best friend. Neither one of them would talk to the other; both were feeling betrayed. Both wanted an apology.

"This is ridiculous," she finally said. "Are you for real? Are you not going to talk for the entire flight?"

Looking at her, Tony pointed at Rhodey. "Why isn't he on Hammer's plane?"

"I was invited," Rhodey said.

"Not by the owner of the plane," Tony said. "And that's bad jetiquette. Guests are not allowed to invite other guests."

Rhodey tried again. "Tony—"

"I'm not a guest," Pepper interrupted. A warning tone crept into her voice.

"Can you tell him I'm not talking to him?" Tony said.

"Then listen," Rhodey said. "What's wrong with you? Do you know that showing classified footage on national television is—?"

"No worse than stabbing your best friend in the back at a Senate hearing?" Tony broke in. "How about a heads-up next time?"

"I gave you the report! I asked you to fact-check it!" Rhodey protested.

"Did not," said Tony.

"He did," asserted Pepper.

Tony glared at both of them. "Like I would even re-member," he said with a wave of his hand. "You still owe me an apology."

"I wouldn't count on it," retorted Rhodey.

Pepper interrupted before the argument could get any worse. "Tony, let's go over your schedule. Can we schedule the call with the secretary-general of the United Nations? It's embarrassing that we missed—"

"Let's talk about my birthday party," Tony said.

Pepper took a deep breath. She wondered how long it would take her to hit the ground if she jumped out of the plane. "I recommend something small, elegant," she began.

"Nope," Tony said. "We're gonna have a huge party."

Pepper let it go and forged ahead. "Monaco," she said. "I think we should cancel." The Monaco Historic Grand Prix car race was one of Tony's favorite rituals.

"Absolutely not," Tony said, exactly as Pepper had anticipated. "I've entered a car in the race." Which Pepper knew, of course. She had seen the financials on the car. Stark Industries had spent a mint on it.

There was silence as the jet began its descent. Rhodey wanted what was best for the United States, and to him the Iron Man suit was the culmination of a long tradition of US military superiority driven by technological innovation. Tony thought Rhodey was just jealous. He wanted a suit. It was that simple.

"Next time," Tony said, "you're flying commercial."

Once he got home, Tony went to work with Jarvis testing new power sources for his chest Arc Reactor, since the palladium fuel cell was proving toxic. Jarvis was trying all sorts of chemical combinations in an effort to improve the formula. But the tests kept failing.

"Rise in palladium levels," Jarvis said. "Toxicity now at twenty-four percent."

Bad news. The purple lines of palladium poisoning spreading from the RT were thicker and longer. Some of them had sprouted smaller lines that wandered off to meet each other, creating a webbed effect.

"You're running out of both time and options," Jarvis said. He had run a number of simulations of potential new fuel cell compounds, and none of them could power the miniaturized Arc Reactor consistently enough to keep the shrapnel in Tony's chest from killing him. "Unfortunately the device that's keeping you alive is also killing you."

While Tony was looking at the ugly lines on his skin, Jarvis warned him that Pepper was approaching. He got his shirt pulled back down just as she tapped her code into the lab door access panel. Tony quickly buttoned up his shirt and picked up one of his new inventions, a Tech-Ball, tossing it around nonchalantly as he turned to meet her.

"Hey," he said before she had a chance to yell at him about something.

But that didn't stop her. "What were you thinking?"

"I'm thinking that I'm busy," he said.

"Did you actually donate our entire modern art collection to the—"

"City after-school program," he finished for her. "It's a fine organization. And it's not our art collection. It's mine."

"I spent ten years curating that collection," Pepper said. "I'm entitled to—" She cut herself off and reset. "Anyway, there're only about eight thousand and eleven things I need to talk to you about."

"Let's start with the Stark Expo."

"It's a huge waste of money," she said.

"It's the only thing that matters," Tony said. He noticed she had a cold and hoped she wouldn't get germs all over his lab...especially if a cold might weaken him while he was fighting the palladium toxicity.

"The Stark Expo is your ego run mad," she said.

That set him off, like it always did, and right away they were arguing about how much Stark Industries money to devote to this or that enterprise or this or that cause. "I don't care anymore," Tony said. "I don't care about the liberal agenda anymore."

"Well, I care—" Pepper started to say, and Tony would never know what she was going to add, because he said, "Fine. You do it."

She either didn't hear him or didn't believe him, because she kept talking. So he kept repeating himself.

"You do it. You run the company."

"I do run it," she said indignantly.

"You're not listening to me. I'm trying to make you CEO! Why won't you listen to me?"

That got her attention.

"I hereby irrevocably appoint you chairman of Stark Industries, effective immediately," Tony said.

She was stunned. She hadn't looked this stunned the first time she'd seen him in the Iron Man armor, all chipped and scarred with bullet and shrapnel holes.

"I've actually given this a lot of thought, considering who a worthy successor would be," Tony said, as he walked over to Dummy, one of his robots, who had just rolled up with a bottle of champagne and two glasses. He popped the cork on the champagne and added, "But then I realized . . . it's you. It's always been you."

Pepper's face ran through six different expressions.

"Are you serious?" she asked. Tony just blinked at her. "You...you are serious," she said.

"Congratulations, Ms. Potts," Tony said, shaking her hand and handing her a glass of champagne.

"I don't know what to think," she said.

"Don't think. Drink," he said. They toasted.

After hours of more failed tests, Tony decided to vent some of his frustration by taking a boxing lesson from his chauffeur. He'd had a boxing ring put into his home gym just for this purpose.

"Cover," Happy said after sticking a jab into Tony's nose. "Don't drop. Hands up. Jab-jab-hook-uppercut-jab."

Eyes watering from the jab, Tony threw the combination. Happy flicked the punches aside and said, "You're dropping your hook. Again."

Tony heard the doorbell ring and a moment later looked up to see Pepper walking into the gym. "The notary's here. Can you please come sign the transfer paperwork?" she called out.

"Great," Tony said.

A young woman he had never seen followed Pepper into the room. "What's your name, young lady?"

"Rushman," she said. "Natalie Rushman."

"Front and center," he said, beckoning her into the ring. He looked at her for a long time. "Give her a lesson, Happy."

Then he hopped out of the ring and went over to sit with Pepper. While she looked on with irritation, he fired up the touchscreen tabletop and pulled up Natalie's résumé from the Stark Industries personnel files. What he saw impressed him.

"Ever box before?" he heard Happy ask Natalie.

"I have," she said.

"What, like kickboxing?" he said, mocking her a little. Hap was a nice guy, but his ego was pretty fragile, especially in the ring.

Tony made no effort to keep the admiration out of his voice as he looked through her résumé—and her modeling photos. This young woman did it all. "Did you see her résumé? Fluent in French, Italian, Russian...*Latin*? Who speaks Latin?"

Pepper, meanwhile, was not so impressed. "No one. It's a dead language. I think you need to meet some new candidates for your assistant," she said.

"I don't have time to meet," Tony said. "I have a feeling about her."

"Mm-hm," she said.

In the ring, Natalie looked back over at them. Happy, pushing his joke a little too far, said, "Lesson number one: Never turn your back on an opponent."

Whenever he said this to Tony, he gave him a little tap on the back of the head. He tried this with Natalie and like she had a sixth sense, she spun, caught his glove, twisted his forearm back, and used his weight to brace her in a leaping martial-arts move. She scissored her legs around his neck and took him down before he even knew what was happening.

"Happy!" Pepper cried out.

Tony got up and ran to the ring. Natalie let go of Happy, who got to his feet and shrugged.

"Slipped," he said.

Natalie got out of the ring and flipped open a tablet. "Mr. Stark, I need your impression," she said.

"Quiet reserve," he said, firing up the flirt engine.

"I mean your fingerprint," she said, showing him the fields on the tablet screen.

"Will that be all, Mr. Stark?"

"Yes," Pepper said. "That will be all, Miss Rushman."

As Natalie walked away with the forms that would make the transfer of Stark Industries to Pepper Potts official, Tony said, "I want her."

"No," Pepper said.

CHAPTER 25

Tony took all of his closest friends and associates to Monaco for the big race. While Happy parked the limousine, Tony and Pepper went into a fancy hotel restaurant to watch the race. Natalie was waiting inside. Tony had overruled Pepper and hired her as his assistant, and he was pleased with his decision so far. Natalie's fluent French came in handy.

As Pepper looked around the room, she saw TVs mounted everywhere, airing prerace coverage. Then she spied Justin Hammer walking across the room. Tony spotted him, too, and sniffed in disgust.

"Anthony!" Hammer boomed on his way to the table. He nodded at Pepper and said, "Is that you? Hey, pal, I'm not the only rich guy here with a fancy car. I just wanted to pop over and congratulate Ms. Potts on her promotion."

"Thank you," Pepper said.

"And you know Christine Everhart? She's doing a spread on me for her magazine."

They bantered for a minute as Tony wondered what Everhart was doing there. She'd already gone after him for making weapons, and inadvertently helped him start to figure out what Obadiah Stane was up to. What was her angle now? Was it that Hammer Industries was trying to pick up the defense contracts Stark had let lapse?

Hammer turned to Tony. "I'm actually hoping to present something at your Expo before it's over," he said.

"Love it!" Tony said. "Just so you know, we're mostly highlighting inventions that *work*. Now if you'll excuse me, I'd like to freshen up before the ball."

Tony zipped out of the room for a quick trip to the head. While in there, he checked his blood toxicity.

It was 53 percent. He'd made it halfway from Awesome to Dead. Tony sighed and considered the fact that it might not have been the best idea he'd ever had to go to Monaco while he was dying of palladium toxicity.

But what the heck? Race day! He planned to enjoy it.

A few minutes later, Hammer was talking to Christine, who he'd been surprised to find out also knew Tony better than she had let on before. But he wasn't going to let that bother him.

"Tony and I," Hammer said. "I love Tony. We're not competitors." Her gaze floated up over his shoulder and at the same time he heard the announcers—in several languages—get excited. Had the race started?

What he saw on the screen made him gasp.

On the screen, in high def, big as life, Tony Stark was getting into the Stark Industries car. He was suited up like the other drivers. He adjusted the steering wheel, shot a thumbs-up at the worldwide audience, then roared off toward the starting line. Although he couldn't understand a word of French, Hammer could hear tone of voice in any language, and he could tell that the French announcers were going crazy. He heard another gasp across the room and noticed that Pepper had just seen the television screen, too. She must not have known about it. She and Tony's hot new assistant were conferring over something. Probably what they were going to do about their attention-seeking nut of a boss. Who wasn't even Pepper's boss anymore. She ought to fire him.

"Can you excuse me?" Christine said.

"Where you going?" Hammer said. "I have some caviar coming."

But she was gone. *That Tony Stark,* thought Hammer, *really knows how to keep a secret.* He did not like that guy at all.

CHAPTER 26

How Ivan loved machines. All machines. In Ivan's veins ran the blood of a born engineer. His father, too, had been destined for engineering greatness. A Stark had derailed that plan. Ivan would get it back on track.

As the race began, Ivan got ready, putting on his harness and two whips. When the time was right, he fired up the whips. The track maintenance worker's coverall he'd been wearing burned off his body from the intense heat coursing through the harness as he strode directly toward the track.

His left-hand whip slashed through the chain-link

fence under the grandstand as if it weren't there, leaving a gouge in the sidewalk. He came to the safety barrier bordering the track, a three-tiered metal railing, and cut through it with two flicks of his wrists as one of the cars thundered by. It was, as the Americans liked to say, showtime.

Viewers in the hotel restaurant couldn't believe what they were seeing. Someone had invaded the track and was using a kind of electrified rope to hack away at the passing cars. He was big, with long, lank hair and a kind of metallic exoskeleton frame that linked his two—ropes? cables? whips?—to a glowing light at the center of his torso.

Cars were swerving and piling up around the invader as they tried to avoid him. "That can't be good," Pepper said. She focused on the invader. He wore what looked suspiciously like a miniaturized Arc Reactor. Where could he have gotten it?

Happy walked in. "What's going on?" he asked.

"Where's the football?" she said quickly. He held it up—an aluminum briefcase lacquered in the same deep red as the Iron Man suit. They had given it the code name "football." It was shackled to his arm.

Pepper told Natalie to get Tony's plane warmed up and ready to take off, and then turned to Happy. "Let's go."

Hurrying to the limo, Pepper said, "Give me the key." Happy held out his arm so she could reach the lock on the football as they ran together out of the hotel and toward the VIP lot.

Left behind in the restaurant, Natalie spoke into her cell phone. "He's going into turn ten." She looked around to make sure no one was watching. "He is extremely vulnerable at the moment," she said.

She was, too. Her support network was a long way off, and it would be very easy for a misunderstanding to escalate, compromising her mission. That could not be allowed to happen.

Natalie held the phone, listening for another moment, and then said, "Understood," and hung up. Then, as Pepper had ordered, she dialed her phone again, to make sure the Stark Industries plane was ready to go when Tony was.

Oblivious to the disruption on the track, Tony was having the time of his life. He had just passed Hammer's car with a grin and a wave.

Suddenly, he saw the cars in front of him veer crazily away from something in the center of the track. Just before one of the cars disappeared in a fireball, Tony could have sworn he saw a man...and something sparking, like live wires.

The fireball cleared, and Tony saw that there *was* a man on the track, walking against the direction of the race. From his hands dangled a pair of whips that glowed and sparked as he flicked them against the concrete.

The car in front of Tony braked and swerved. Tony stayed behind it, using it as a shield. A flickering line of energy shot out and split the car in half. The two pieces, spitting vapors and flame, tumbled into the crash barrier. Now Tony really stood on the brakes. He hauled on the steering wheel, felt the car skid, and watched in what felt like slow motion as the man flicked one of the whips toward Tony's car.

The whip sheared through the chassis and split the car

into two pieces, which flipped and slid along the track, coming to a stop upside down. Tony popped the steering wheel loose and tossed it out onto the track so that he could wriggle out of the driver's seat. His helmet had cracked in the crash, and he stripped it off. The remains of his car rested between him and the guy with the whips and the metal exoskeleton, but right then he reached the wreck and slashed it into small pieces, shouting in Russian. Tony waited for just the right moment, then grabbed hold of the nearest bit of wreckage and swung it at the back of his head.

Tony put everything he had into the swing. It was a good one. The blow landed solidly...but had no visible effect.

The man roared like an animal and slashed at Tony, but Tony was already off and running for cover. All he saw were pieces of race cars, beautiful machines turned into expensive junk.

One car lay upside down at an angle that would provide brief cover, leaking gas all over the track. Tony had an idea. He dove under the car, yanked off the gas cap, and scrambled away from the splash of fuel. He got clear just as the man was close enough to strike.

The superheated whip slashed down through the car's

engine and into the pool of fuel on the track surface. The explosion that followed blew the car to unrecognizable pieces and sent Tony pinwheeling into a wall of hay bales at the edge of the track. He got to his feet and looked back toward the dissipating fireball.

There was the man, walking through the flames as if they weren't there and coming toward Tony as though he were the only thing in the world that mattered.

"I see Tony!" Happy cried out. The thing about Monaco was the race was right through downtown, so the hotel was literally close enough that they almost could have run faster. Happy had just crashed through the gate and onto the track—going the wrong way. There were hulks of destroyed cars, pit crews running onto the track to save drivers, spectators rushing up and down the stands in waves. There was fire on the track, everywhere.

Happy lost sight of Tony. A fireball on the track hid everything. Happy accelerated that way.

There was Tony again.

Happy took in the situation all at once. Tony was half-buried in a collapsed pile of hay bales on the inside of the crash barriers, trying to get up. A big area of the track near Tony was on fire. Through the fire came the big nutcase with the laser whips, cracking them on the pavement and grinning.

There was one thing to do, and Happy did it. He cut the wheel hard and hammered down on the brakes, sending the limo into a drift and smashing the bad guy into the railing with the back end. The limo slammed hard into the crash barrier, crumpling the railings and setting off the air bags. It had pinned the guy to the wall.

What to do next? Happy wondered. His shattered window fell apart and he noticed the boss approaching the limo. Pepper was screaming at Tony to get in the car, Tony was shouting back at her to give him the case.

Happy, meanwhile, kept gunning the engine to hold the maniac with the whips at bay. As Tony reached for the case, the car lurched. The man reared up from behind it and, with a barbaric yell, whistled one of his whips past Tony's head, splitting the nearest door in two. The second whip tore through the armored hood of the car as if it were aluminum foil. Tony spun away. The man slashed at the car to free himself. He hacked away at the hood and the engine compartment, his whips even slicing through to shred the seats into the backseat.

From the limo, Pepper called out, "Tony!" She slid the football across the slick pavement in his direction. Then she and Happy just ducked and hoped that Tony would take care of the situation before the car, with them in it, was carved up to scraps.

Incredibly, the lunatic, who was wearing an RT on his chest, had hacked away enough of the front end of the car that he was almost loose. He shoved free and stalked through the wreckage after Tony.

Tony entered a code into a pad next to the football's handle. It chirped its acceptance. He opened the case and placed one foot in either half. A light, portable version of the Iron Man suit, the Mark V, built itself from the boots up around Tony's body. It wasn't the same as the full apparatus, but it was still a formidable piece of body armor.

The Mark V finished assembling itself just in time. The first crack from an energized whip left deep scoring in the suit's shoulder. Tony dodged the next several swings and goggled at the RT on the man's chest. *How is that possible?* Tony thought. Even the Department of Defense had no idea how Arc Reactor tech worked. Who was this person who had just shown up in Monaco and started wrecking the place with RT-powered whips?

A whip sparked across Tony's torso, coming dangerously

close to his own RT. Tony grabbed the arm holding the whip and flung the man into the smoking wreckage of two cars. When he got up, Tony had powered up the repulsors, and fired.

The man deflected the blast with one of the whips. That was something Tony had never seen before. In his brief moment of surprise, he left himself open. The maniac flicked one of them around his neck and jerked him to the ground. But that was where he overreached. Tony caught the whips, feeling them short out various circuits in the gauntlets. He swung the guy up and around, and drove him into the pavement. Then, before he could get up, Tony tore the RT from the whip wielder's chest and looked at it. He couldn't quite believe what he saw.

Police swarmed the downed lunatic, who laughed the whole time they were dragging him away. "You lose," he said over and over, in an accent. "You lose."

CHAPTER 27

By the time Tony walked into the local police station, he'd run some preliminary tests on the RT recovered from Whiplash—as the media had already named him. The results were startlingly similar to Tony's own design.

In the hallway, he found a French prison official, who recognized him. "Who is he?"

"We are not sure yet. His first name is Ivan. We assume he's Russian. We're not even sure he speaks English. He hasn't said a word since he got here." The official let Tony into the holding cell where a manacled Ivan sat, wearing only his underwear with his back to the door. His skin was a gallery of tattoos.

"Pretty decent tech," he said, and meant it. "If you'd gone to double cycles you'd get better yields. Some other things you could have done. Little refinement here and there, you could make yourself a paycheck somewhere. North Korea, China."

He walked around so Ivan could see him. "Where'd you get it?"

Vanko looked at him with no trace of fear. "You come from a family of thieves and butchers. And now you guilty men tried to rewrite your own history."

A family of thieves. Tony stored away that statement. What did this Ivan know about his family? "Speaking of thieves, where did you get this design?" he asked.

"My father. Anton Vanko," Ivan said reverently.

"Never heard of him."

"My father is the reason you're alive."

"I'm alive because you had a shot and you took it and you missed," Tony said.

Vanko laughed, a sound like rocks rubbing against each other. "If you could make God bleed, people would cease to believe in Him. There will be blood in the water, the sharks will come. All I have to do is sit back and watch as the world consumes you."

The prison officials opened the door and let him know his visit was over.

"Where will you be watching this world consume me? A prison cell. I'll send you a bar of soap," Tony said, and headed for the door.

"Hey, Tony," Ivan said. "Palladium in the chest. It's a painful way to die."

Tony stopped. How did Vanko know? For a moment Tony almost turned to ask. Then he decided, no. That's giving him too much power. Using palladium wasn't the hardest part of making an RT, and Vanko could have guessed that was what was making him sick.

But now Tony knew that even strangers could tell he looked sick. He had to do something about it. Time was running out.

"He's completely unhinged. He thinks of the Iron Man weapon as a toy," Senator Stern was complaining on TV while Tony flew back to the United States with Pepper.

"Mute," he said, and sat down, irritated that Stern was still after him. Stark Industries was taking a beating in the press, and the company's shareholders weren't happy about the new directions Tony had taken it. They all wanted him to sell the Iron Man tech, which he thought was nuts. "They should be giving me a medal," he grumbled to Pepper. "Here." He set a covered plate down and then uncovered it.

"What's that?" Pepper asked.

"Inflight meal," Tony said.

"You made that?"

"Yeah, where do you think I've been for the last three hours?" He tried to sell the joke, but there was an expression on Pepper's face that told him she was seeing through it.

"Tony," Pepper said. "What are you not telling me?"

He thought about telling her. He wanted to tell her. In the end, though, he decided not to. She needed to run Stark Industries, and he needed to figure out how to refuel his RT without killing himself. Division of labor.

"Let's cancel my birthday party and . . . let's go to Venice," he said.

Pepper shook her head. "Now? With things the way they are? I think as CEO, I need to show up."

"As CEO, you can go on a retreat," Tony said. "Get away. Recharge our batteries..."

"Not everybody runs on batteries, Tony." She gave him a sad smile, and he had no answer. Because the way things looked, he wasn't going to be running on a battery for much longer, either.

Three hours later, a guard arrived at Vanko's cell door and set a tray of food on the shelf built into the bars. He made eye contact with Vanko, then walked away. Ivan looked at the food. There was a note. *Enjoy the potatoes*, it said. In Russian.

He picked up the potatoes. They were a single, smooth blob. He turned it over...and set into the underside of the blob was a digital time.

Ivan put it all together. At that moment, the guard returned. He guided another prisoner in and shut the door. This new prisoner was Ivan's size, had Ivan's hair...and his prison jumpsuit bore the number 6219.

Just like Ivan's.

He jumped the new prisoner and smashed his head into the sink before dropping his limp body to the ground.

The guard passed by a third time, and now he set a key on the shelf where he'd left the food.

Ivan planted the explosive charge on the wall. It started counting. :35, :34 …

He had plenty of time to unlock the door and walk down the hall before the explosive went off. Whatever remained of the other prisoner 6219, no one would look very hard. Vanko ducked into a stairwell. Alarms shrieked and prison guards were everywhere. Two of them grabbed him and hooded him before dragging him out and throwing him into a van. It was dark inside, and hot. But Ivan Vanko was free.

Or would be soon.

At the end of the ride was a hangar with a private jet, and a table set for two. At the table sat an American in a white suit. "There he is!" the American called out. He had Ivan brought to the table, his handcuffs removed. The tablecloth was softer than any fabric he had ever owned. The American was eating ice cream that he said had been flown in from California. Ice cream, flown across oceans.

"I'm such a huge fan of yours," he said. "My name is Justin Hammer. I'd like to do some business with you." Over dessert, which Hammer ate first, he kept talking. "The way you stood up to Tony Stark there, in front of God and everybody... wow. That spoke to me. Because— if you don't mind me saying—you don't just go up and try to kill a guy. You go after his legacy. That's what you kill."

Interesting, thought Ivan. He had thoughts along the same lines, although he would have been happy just to kill Stark, too. "You need my resources," Hammer said. "You need a benefactor. I'd like to be that guy."

Ah well. This man wanted to give him a job to kill Tony Stark?

That was fine. Except for one thing.

"I want my bird," Ivan said.

It took him some time to make himself understood, but when he had assurances that Irina would be on her way from Moscow, Ivan relaxed a little. What would come next, he did not know. It did not matter. What mattered was the humiliation of Tony Stark.

CHAPTER 28

Back at Stark Industries, Rhodey had arrived to talk to Tony. Pepper and Natalie were fielding media calls. "Where is he?" Rhodey asked.

"Downstairs," Pepper said, over Natalie's objections. She waved him down to the lab.

He got to the bottom of the stairs and peered through the glass walls. Tony sat in one of his cars, staring at his virtual desktop. He wasn't looking at Iron Man schematics or breakdowns of engines, though. He was pulling gigabytes of old video footage, photographs, scanned-in reports. . . . Rhodey couldn't quite see how they fit together, and he wouldn't find out until he asked, so he knocked.

Tony glanced up and let him in.

"Tony, you have to get upstairs and get on top of this situation right now. I've been on the phone all day talking them out of rolling tanks up to your front door and taking these suits," Rhodey said.

Tony didn't answer. He just stared off into space, barely acknowledging Rhodey's presence.

"You said it would be twenty years before someone else would figure out your technology. Well, guess what? Somebody had it yesterday," Rhodey said. "It's not theoretical anymore."

He looked more closely at Tony and thought to himself that Tony looked like a man with one foot in the grave. "Are you listening to me? You okay?"

Tony got up out of the car and Rhodey helped him to his desk. Tony took out his RT and showed Rhodey the smoking depleted palladium cell.

"You had this in your body?" Rhodey said. He was starting to understand what was behind Tony's recent behavior. "And how about that high-tech crossword puzzle on your neck?" he added, pointing to the purplish lines spreading up from under the collar of Tony's shirt.

"Road rash," Tony said, but Rhodey could see his heart wasn't in the joke. Tony was dying. The RT was poisoning him.

"You don't have to do this alone," Rhodey said. There were plenty of doctors who could help...weren't there?

Tony shook his head and started to get back to work. "You have to trust me. Contrary to popular belief, I know exactly what I'm doing."

Rhodey watched his old friend for a long time after that, but there was really nothing else to say.

"Here they are," Hammer said to Vanko as they walked into the main Hammer Industries research lab. "Very excited. They're combat-ready. I might have rushed the prototype...." Hammer broke off as Vanko dug right into his heavily encrypted software and cracked it before Hammer could even ask someone to get him a password. *Skills,* thought Hammer. This guy had them.

Then he just watched as Vanko climbed a stepladder and started pulling pieces of one of the drone soldiers off. They were designed to accommodate a pilot, which was a tricky engineering problem.

"What you want them for?" Vanko said from the top of the ladder.

"Long term, I want them to get me into the Pentagon. But for now I want to make Iron Man look like an antique."

"I can do that, no problem," Vanko said with a throaty laugh.

"Hey, this is our guy!" Hammer said. "I had a feeling."

Natalie helped Tony get ready for the party. He was exhausted and depressed and inclined to cancel the whole thing...but that wasn't the Tony Stark people wanted to see.

"I should cancel the party," Tony said.

She nodded. "Probably."

"Because it sends the wrong message."

She looked over her shoulder at him. "Inappropriate."

Oh my, Tony thought. They looked at each other for a long moment. Natalie applied a little lotion to the bruises on Tony's face. "Hypothetical question," Tony said. "Bit odd. If this was your last birthday party, how would you celebrate it?"

Looking him right in the eye, Natalie said, "I'd do whatever I wanted to do. With whoever I wanted to do it with."

Good advice, Tony thought. He decided not to cancel the party after all.

While the celebrities and other guests started to arrive downstairs, Tony was still up in his room. He had asked Jarvis to run another test on his RT, and the results were not encouraging. Tony stood there stewing until he heard Natalie coming out of one of the walk-in closets with an outrageously bright-colored tie. She looped it around his neck and started tying it. "Voilà," she said, buttoning his collar and tightening the tie perfectly. "I'll go downstairs and make sure everything is ready," she said.

"You're a gem," Tony said.

A while later, Pepper walked into the party, taking in the huge crowd and the loud music. She sighed and made her way through the packed house, looking for Tony. She found him swaying by the DJ booth, wearing one of the Iron Man suits with the faceplate up. A cheering crowd rocked out in front of him.

This was too much. She turned right around and headed for the door just as Rhodey was coming from the driveway. "Hey, Pepper," he said.

They both looked into the house and saw Tony, falling down and lurching back to his feet. "I can't...I just don't know what to do, Rhodey," Pepper said. She bit her lip.

Rhodey was furious. "I'm gonna—"

Before he could go on, Pepper stopped him. "Let me handle it," she said.

"I just stuck my neck out for this guy. You handle it or I'm going to," Rhodey said.

Pepper headed for the stage, where Tony was about to give some kind of speech. She took the mike away from him and said, "We all thank you so much for such a wonderful night." Tony started to talk to her away from the mike. She got him to agree and he took the mike back.

Then he said, "She's right. The party's over. The after-party starts in fifteen minutes...and if anybody doesn't like it, there's the door!" He pointed at the door and the repulsor in that gauntlet discharged, blasting the glass door into a million shards.

The crowd went wild. Feeding off their energy, Tony started shooting other things with the repulsors. Rhodey watched for another minute. Pepper stood where he had left her, shocked.

Decision time, Rhodey thought. He was about to do something that Tony might never forgive, but for the life of him, Rhodey couldn't figure out what else to do.

He remembered Tony saying that what people needed was not more suits like his but more guys like him. Right now, Rhodey thought that one Tony Stark was plenty. More than enough, in fact.

But one Iron Man suit was not enough at all. Not nearly.

A few minutes later, Tony was rocking out, shooting fruit out of the air with his unibeam and riding a wave of pure abandon. Now this was a party. Natalie had been right!

Then a voice cut through the cheering. "I'm only gonna say this once."

Everyone turned to see Colonel James Rhodes in a gleaming steel version of the Iron Man suit. They fell silent.

"Get out," he said.

Everyone headed for the door, leaving Tony and Rhodey

facing each other down. "You don't deserve to wear one of these," Rhodey said. "Shut it down."

Tony turned to the DJ. "Give me a fat beat for when I beat my friend's head in," he said.

Then it was on. Rhodey grappled with Tony and with a thrust-assisted spring, Tony drove both of them backward. Their combined weight and momentum was too much for the wall, and they blew through it into the gym. Panicked guests streamed out of the house and gathered in the yard to watch.

They grappled in the boxing ring. Tony uprooted a corner post and swung; Rhodey got one of his own, and the two of them went at it like broadsword-wielding medieval knights until the posts broke. They crashed up through the ceiling, then back down into the living room, exchanging punches like heavyweights late in a match when all the technique was gone and both were running on pure rage. Happy led Pepper out into the back of the house. Natalie ran the other way, reaching for her phone.

Then Tony put Rhodey down with a final combination and a body slam into the base of the living room fountain.

He turned to see everyone watching.

Taking pictures of the complete lunatic he had become. He roared at them, just wanting them out. They ran.

Rhodey got up and leveled Tony from behind. Tony got up and they faced each other, repulsor gauntlets leveled. "You got what it takes to be a war machine?" Tony asked.

"Put it down," Rhodey said.

"Take your shot, then!" Tony shouted.

"Put it down!" Rhodey repeated.

They fired simultaneously. The repulsor beams collided and lit off an explosion that blew out the back wall of the house in a huge ball of flame.

When it was over, Tony and Rhodey stood looking at each other. There was nothing else to say. Rhodey fired the boot rockets and lifted away into the night sky.

He flew away from the ruins of Tony's house in the suit toward Edwards Air Force Base, knowing that his actions would change the nature of their friendship—maybe even end it. Forever.

He had wanted to believe Tony's spiel about using the suit for the right reasons and protecting it from those who shouldn't have access to that kind of technology. But Tony had let them all down. Rhodey could be sad and disappointed about it, but he knew his duty.

CHAPTER 29

I t was morning. Tony didn't like mornings, as a general rule. Warnings from Jarvis about palladium poisoning, and knowing Rhodey had betrayed him, made this particular morning worse. The only thing making it bearable was the box of jelly doughnuts he was currently stuffing into his face. While sitting in a much larger doughnut outside a landmark bakery in Los Angeles.

"Sir," someone called from below. "I'm going to have to ask you to exit the doughnut."

Tony looked down. The speaker was a stern-looking man with an eye patch and a black leather jacket.

"Oh, brother," Tony said. "Didn't I kick you out of my house once already?" This same guy—Nick Fury, that was his name—had showed up wanting to talk about some kind of secret project. Avengers something. Tony had plenty of secret projects of his own going on. He didn't need anyone else's.

But he could use a cup of coffee. He dropped down and they went inside to a table.

"I told you I don't want to join your super secret boy band," he said.

"Oh, no no no, I remember, you do everything yourself. How's that working out for you?"

Tony evaded the question. "I'm sorry, I don't want to get off on the wrong foot. Do I look at the patch or the eye? I'm not sure if you're real or ..."

"I am very real," Fury said. "I'm the realest person you're ever gonna meet."

"Just my luck. Where's the staff here?" Tony asked.

Fury pulled down Tony's collar to look at the marks on his neck. "That's not looking too good," he said.

"Been worse," Tony said, even though it wasn't true.

Then Natalie came walking up. She was wearing a bodysuit in the same design as Fury's trench coat, with visible S.H.I.E.L.D. emblems on it. "We've secured the perimeter. But I don't think we should hold it for too much longer."

She'd infiltrated him. Looking at her, Tony said, "You're... fired."

"That's not up to you," she said, and sat next to Fury across from him in the booth.

"Tony, meet Agent Romanoff," Fury said.

This was too much. S.H.I.E.L.D. was putting the hard sell on Tony, and he didn't like it. "What do you want from me?"

"You've become a problem for me," Fury said. He went on, and as Tony tried to ignore him, Natalie—Agent Romanoff—came around the table and stuck a needle in his neck.

"Ow! What did you just do to me?" Tony said.

"What did we just do for you," Fury corrected. "Lithium dioxide. It'll take the edge off the palladium poisoning. We're trying to get you back to work."

"I've tried every conceivable combination and permutation to replace palladium in the RT. Believe me."

"Well, I'm here to tell you you haven't tried them all," Fury said.

"We were going to have this conversation sometime," said the bald-headed man. "Now seems like a good time."

Tony shook his head. "Not interested. I have a lot on my mind." He turned his attention back to his doughnuts.

After a while, Fury put something on the table while still looking Tony in the eye. Tony glanced down and saw a roll of sixteen-millimeter film and a manila envelope. He opened the envelope. Inside it was a black-and-white photograph of a fortyish man taken sometime in the 1950s or early '60s, if the surrounding tech was anything to judge by.

"Who's this?" he asked.

"Anton Vanko," Fury said. "He worked with your dad."

Whiplash's father! This was a curveball. "I didn't see this in my files, or my dad's" was all Tony could think of to say.

"Because it was in *our* files." Fury paused to let that sink in. "Your father saw the future. Which is why he came and worked for us."

"What do you mean?" Tony asked.

"Sometimes people are born before the world is ready for them," Fury replied. "Leonardo da Vinci invented the helicopter before anyone had even predicted flight. Howard Stark made a few predictions, too. He was just born way too early to execute them. The world had to play catch-up."

Tony knew his father was a genius. But to hear Howard Stark mentioned in the same breath as Leonardo da Vinci... Tony wasn't sure how to react, and he also wasn't sure what Fury meant the comparison to convey.

Fury tapped a finger on the film canister and said, "And now the world has just caught up." Fury stood. "That's where you come in. And if you don't, someone else will."

CHAPTER 30

Justin Hammer installed Ivan in a secret laboratory in California. He could hardly believe his good luck. One week earlier, he had been working in two rooms with illegally tapped power and a computer he'd scrounged from someone else's trash. Now he was looking at an entire floor of top-quality computers and tools. He had everything he needed for smelting, machining, welding, wiring, plating, microwave circuit manufacture.... *If my father had been given the use of a lab like this,* Ivan thought, *he would have changed the world.*

Stark had taken away that glory. Ivan Vanko would reclaim it.

Much of the lab's floor space was taken up by long rows of gleaming metal drones, humanoid in shape and visibly armed. His task was to outfit each of them with an RT. But before he could do that, he had needed to know how they were put together. So he'd taken one apart, down to each circuit, and he had realized that they would work better with one thing removed: the pilot.

So since Hammer had left him to work a few days before, Ivan had reconfigured each of the armored suits into drones that could be operated remotely and independently without a pilot. Now they were much more efficient, much more deadly. The drones were his soldiers. They still needed some work, but they would do nicely.

Hammer, however, didn't agree. When he stopped into the lab to see how Ivan was doing, Hammer threw a fit when he saw that there was no longer space for a human operator. "This isn't a helmet," he said, holding one of the drones' heads. "It's a head. What are you doing, Ivan?"

"Drone better," Ivan said.

"Why is drone better?"

"People make problem," Ivan said.

Hammer didn't like this. "I need suits. The government wants suits. That's what the people want. That's what's going to make 'em happy."

Ivan just looked at him. Hammer handed the drone head back to him. "These drones better steal the show, Ivan," he said. "They better rock my world."

Ivan said nothing, and Hammer left him alone again, which was what he had wanted all along. Hammer still thought he was in charge, but now this was Ivan Vanko's lab and he would do things his way.

One of these drones, Ivan thought, *will be the last thing Tony Stark ever sees.*

Unless—and this was the only more desirable possibility—the last thing Stark saw was the apparatus Ivan Vanko was building for himself.

Sitting outside his ruined house, Tony talked with Fury because Fury wouldn't leave him alone. Also, the shot had done him some good, and Tony wondered what other tricks Fury might have up his sleeve.

"That thing in your chest is based on an unfinished technology," Fury was saying. "Howard was onto something big, so big that it was going to make the nuclear reactor look like a triple-A battery."

"Just him, or was Anton Vanko part of it?"

"Anton was the other side of that coin. Anton saw it as a way to get rich. When your father found out he was trying to sell the tech to other parties, he had him deported. Vanko spent the next twenty years in a vodka-fueled rage. Not the best environment for a kid...but you met him already."

Tony remembered Ivan slashing at him with the plasma whips. No wonder he was so angry. "So what do you want me to do?"

"Your father always said you were the one who could create the future," Fury said. "That means you can solve the riddle of your heart."

Tony did not believe this for a single moment. "Listen, I don't know what you heard, but my dad wasn't my biggest fan. The happiest day of his life was when he shipped me off to boarding school."

"That's not true," Fury said.

"Oh really? Then you must have known him better than I did."

"As a matter of fact, I did," Fury said. "He was one of the founding members of S.H.I.E.L.D."

"What?"

But Fury was done talking. Two of his men brought Tony a metal crate. "I'm leaving Natasha here with her cover intact," he said. Pointing to another S.H.I.E.L.D. agent, he added, "And you know Agent Coulson. Remember: I got my eye on you," Fury said. Then he left Tony to work. Agent Romanoff informed him he was cut off from the outside world.

"If you attempt to leave, I will Tase you and watch TV while you drool into the carpet," Coulson said.

"I think I got it," Tony said. After that, there was nothing to do but open the crate.

At Edwards Air Force Base, a staff sergeant gathered a select group of the air force's best and brightest combat engineers around the Mark II armor. Rhodey, with Major Allen at his left, stood next to it.

"What you will be weaponizing," Rhodey told the assembled team, "is a flying prototype of the Iron Man Mark II, for the purposes of an offensive footing."

"Yes, sir," the engineers said, more or less in unison.

They approached it, wrenches and screwdrivers in hand. One of them picked up the helmet.

As the engineers got to work, Justin Hammer slammed in through the machine shop door. "You have got to be kidding me!" he exclaimed. "I got here as quickly as I could."

Rhodey shook hands with Hammer and said, "You think you can hook it up?"

Hammer's men were bringing in an array of crates and setting them near the Mark II. He winked and popped the lid off the closest crate while his men opened the rest. They contained a huge array of weapons.

Rhodey looked it all over: Gatling cannons, mini-rockets, even what looked like a miniature cruise missile. "I think I'll take it," he said, after a brief—and calculated—pause.

"Which one?" Hammer asked.

"All of 'em," Rhodey said on his way out of the hangar. He didn't like what was happening. His commanders wanted to display the new suit at the Stark Expo, and Rhodey thought it should be kept as a last resort. It wasn't something to make theater out of. But that wasn't up to him. He was a soldier, and he would follow orders.

The crate Fury left was full of Howard Stark's records and personal items. There were newspaper clippings, blueprints, sketches, all kinds of stuff...including a roll of sixteen-millimeter film. As it happened, Tony was a collector of outdated technologies—including an old sixteen-millimeter film projector. Tony spooled the film and started it up. It was an outtake from a promotional film for the Expo, the same one Tony had shown a couple of weeks before.

"Everything is achievable through technology," Tony's father began again. "I'm Howard Stark, and everything you'll need for the future can be found right here...." He trailed off and started over again, repeating that line. In the background, a six-year-old version of Tony appeared, fooling around with a scale model of the Stark Expo. "Tony, what are you doing there?" Howard chased him away and started over again, repeating his first line. Howard kept forgetting his lines and ad-libbing.

Tony started to ignore the film as he leafed through some of his father's notebooks, dense with mathematical formulas and lab notations. Then, from the screen, his father said, "Tony. You're too young to understand some of this, so I thought I'd put it on film for you."

That got his attention.

"I built this for you," his father went on. "And someday you'll realize it represents a lot more than just people's inventions. This is the key to the future. I'm limited by the technology of my time, but one day you'll figure this out, and then you'll change the world. What is and always will be my greatest creation...is you."

Tony looked harder now. He played the film back, his father's words ringing in his mind....

And there it was!

Tony jammed a pen into one of the projector's spindles, stopping the film. Focusing on the puzzle his father had sent him, Tony wound the filmstrip back manually, frame by frame, until he saw it again.

The key was in the Expo model. Something about the arrangement of the buildings...it went with what his father was saying. Tony wound the film slowly enough that he could see each of the still frames and check the tiny differences between them.

There. Tony leaned forward, tracing his finger along the edge of the frame.

At the moment Howard Stark was saying "the future," the Expo's structures looked as though they were arranged in a way that almost might be ... elemental.

Tony got up and headed for his car. *Got it, Dad,* he thought.

CHAPTER 31

To get his model of the Stark Expo, he had to go to his office. That meant he had to talk to Pepper, which did not go well. Tony took everything she handed out. He deserved all the anger. Then she left and he hauled the model out of his car and down into the lab. "Jarvis, I need a rendering of this," he said.

When that was done, Tony flipped it vertical, stripped all the extra stuff out of it, and lo and behold...he was looking at an atom that did not exist in the real world.

"Twenty years later, Dad, and you're still taking me to school," he said. But he wasn't angry anymore. Seeing his father talking to him through the film had affected him in ways it would take a long time to process.

"That element will be an adequate replacement for palladium," Jarvis said. "However, it is impossible to synthesize here."

"Then we're going into remodeling mode," Tony said.

Three hours later, he was ready.

Manipulating elements and breaking their chemical bonds to each other took a lot of energy, so Tony had rigged up a crazy system to ramp up enough power. The parts included a high-energy laser array; a set of mirrors designed to focus the lasers on a single, specific point in space; a cube of pure glass whose position in space included the specific focal point of the set of mirrors; and, finally, a centrifuge designed to initiate high-energy chemical reactions. The system was complicated, but so was molecular engineering. It was, more or less, a particle accelerator, but the output would be a beam of energy at a certain frequency that would—if his math was right—create the new element.

He ran checks, and everything seemed ready. The only

thing left to do was run the experiment and see if he could create a new molecule in his basement.

He had to pause because Agent Coulson came in to give him a mild hard time for leaving...and to notify Tony that he'd been reassigned to New Mexico. "Land of enchantment," Tony commented, remembering the state motto.

"So they say," Coulson said. He started to leave and then paused. "We need you."

"More than you know," Tony said.

Coulson gave him a tolerant smile and left the lab.

The laser array flared to life, first in a deep red and then modulating in frequency well up into the ultraviolet range.

Time to really see if he could make a new element. "Fingers crossed," Tony said.

The centrifuge hit its target acceleration. A laser beam burst out of the lens and deflected through a prism. Tony turned the beam slowly, burning away various bits of furniture and parts of the wall, until it targeted the focus plate of raw material he was hoping to transform into the heart of a new Arc Reactor.

When the laser hit it, the whole piece flared to life. Even through his goggles, Tony couldn't look at it directly. Energy crackled around it like a concentrated local burst of lightning.

Tony held his breath. The lasers had gone cold, the accelerator had spun down to silence, and the circular focus plate had a fiercely glowing triangle at its center.

"That was easy," he said.

"Congratulations, sir. You've created a new element," Jarvis said.

Tony put it into the existing Arc Reactor. It beeped and flickered. "Sir, the reactor has accepted the new core. I will begin running diagnostics."

Tony exhaled, long and slow. *Well,* he thought. *I guess I owe Fury a thank-you card.*

Hammer called Ivan to tell him he was playing golf with Senator Stern. "I'm going to bring him by. What can you show him?"

"Drones not ready."

"What do you mean, not ready?"

"Will be ready for Expo. Not for demonstration."

"What can you do now?"

"No fly, no shoot."

"Well, what can you make them do?"

"Can salute."

Hammer hung up. Ivan got back to work. He had lied to Hammer. The drones were fine. But he was working on something he didn't want Hammer to see...the next generation of his plasma whips. Because he had his own plans for the Stark Expo.

Thirty minutes later Hammer came into the lab with a pair of his goons. They took Ivan's shoes. They took his pillows. Hammer insulted him.

And they took the bird.

"You feel bad?" Hammer asked. "Good, because I feel bad! But you got lucky, because I got a piece of Stark technology for the Expo. It's going to make your drones look like paperweights. How does that make you feel?"

Ivan just sat there. His moment would come. He was not afraid of men like Justin Hammer, because they were too stupid to be afraid of men like him.

The rest of it he could forgive, but not taking the bird. She was innocent.

"I'm gonna leave now and go to the Expo. These guys are going to be your babysitters. They are not to be trifled with. When I get back, we're going to renegotiate the terms of your contract."

A few hours' work produced a functioning new triangular Arc Reactor and a sleeve that would fit the new RT inside the existing socket in Tony's chest. He was running preliminary tests when Jarvis said, "Call incoming."

Tony set the new RT down. "What do you want?" he said, not caring who it was on the other end.

Then he heard the voice of Ivan Vanko.

"Tony. Good advice about double cycles," he said.

"You sound pretty sprightly for a dead man."

"You too. Today the true history of the Stark name will be written."

"Jarvis, where is he?" Tony asked quietly.

Vanko didn't hear. "What your father did to my family forty years ago, I do to you in forty minutes."

"Sounds good. Let's get together and hash it out."

Jarvis pinpointed Vanko's location.

That could only mean one thing. He was headed for the Expo if they couldn't cut him off first.

No time for testing. He stood up and put the new RT in. It blazed in his chest and for a moment Tony thought it was killing him. "Whoa," he said. The power of the new element surged through the connection between the RT and his heart. Was he glowing? It was hard to tell, he couldn't really see....

CHAPTER 32

Agent Romanoff was sick of playing Natalie, but Fury had said Pepper Potts was not to know of her under-cover infiltration. So here she was, with a headset and a clipboard, waiting around the entrance to the Tent of Tomorrow for Pepper to show up. Hammer's demonstration was due to start in five minutes.

The Tent of Tomorrow was actually an open auditorium space under a soaring glass roof, with a high-tech stage and an even higher-tech backstage setup. The backstage area swarmed with Hammer Industries tech personnel making last-minute adjustments to their demonstration.

The seats were packed except a few chairs reserved for VIPs.

Romanoff scanned the crowd again.

"Ms. Potts!" she called out. Pepper and Happy saw her and started in her direction. "I'll show you to your seats," Romanoff said. Her phone rang, and she answered it without looking at the number. "Natalie Rushman."

"Ivan's up to something," Tony said before she finished answering. "He called me from a lab."

There was the barest of pauses. "Yes, Ms. Potts has just arrived," Romanoff said briskly. "Okay. I'll be right there."

She must already be at the Expo, Tony thought as Natasha hung up. *Good.* Maybe she could get S.H.I.E.L.D. personnel to slow Whiplash down until Tony could suit up and get there.

CHAPTER 33

Back at the Expo, Pepper watched Justin Hammer take the stage and begin his show. He danced out to a funky intro, then got a little more serious after his first welcoming remarks.

"In a truly perfect world, men and women of the United States military would never have to set foot on the battlefield again." Music built, and Hammer stepped around to the lip of the stage. "Ladies and gentlemen, today we cross the threshold into . . . a perfect world."

Red, white, and blue smoke erupted around the stage as four lines of armored soldiers marched into the Tent of

Tomorrow and stopped in formation along the sides of the stage. An announcer boomed out the name of each branch of service as its members appeared in turn: "Army! Navy! Air Force! Marines!"

When they met in their formation, slowly and in unison, the thirty-two soldiers pivoted and raised their right arms in salute.

And that was when Pepper—along with everyone else in the Tent of Tomorrow—realized that these were not armored soldiers.

They were walking, synchronized, remote-controlled drones.

Pepper had never heard a noise as loud as the roar of approval from the crowd. Each group of drones represented a service branch. The air force drones were equipped to fly, with winglike additions to every limb and active control surfaces along their backs. The army drones were squat and loaded with heavy weaponry. The marine contingent looked leaner and faster, ready to storm a beach right then and there. And the navy drones stood streamlined and potent, midnight blue, bristling with missiles.

"Better than some cheerleaders, let me tell you. But today I am proud to present to you the Variable Threat Response Battle Suit, and its pilot, James Rhodes!"

From under the stage, a platform rose to reveal War Machine, shining silver in the spotlights. Pepper caught her breath. A million flashbulbs went off. The appearance of War Machine took the crowd's collective breath away.

Then, with timing so precise that Pepper later would wonder whether he had planned his arrival this way, Iron Man rocketed down through the hole in the roof in his new Mark VI suit, complete with a new triangular RT.

Whatever Hammer felt at seeing Tony crash his big party, he was a showman, and he rolled with it. "And that's not all!" Hammer said. "Here, ladies and gentlemen, is our very special surprise guest: Iron Man!"

Tony waved to the crowd while he popped open a communications channel from his heads-up display to Rhodey's heads-up display inside the War Machine suit. "There are civilians present," Rhodey said. "Let's not do this right now."

"All these people are in danger," Tony said. "We've got to get them out of here. I think Hammer's working with Vanko."

"Vanko's alive?" Rhodey said incredulously.

Tony turned to Hammer. "Where's Vanko?"

"What are you doing here, man?" Hammer snapped.

He looked like a guy whose girlfriend's ex had just crashed his party.

Then Rhodey said, "Whoa, whoa," and as Tony looked back at him, the War Machine armor's shoulder Gatling cannon locked into firing position. Aimed at Tony.

"Get out of here! Go! This whole system's been compromised!" Rhodey shouted.

Vanko, thought Tony. The drones, all thirty-two of them, also went into battle-ready postures.

"Let's take it outside," Tony said, and shot off into the air.

A fusillade of drone fire followed him. A moment later, so did War Machine and the air force drones. "Tony, I have target lock," Rhodey said.

"On what?"

"On you!" Cannon fire raked Tony's armor as he jerked and wove over the Expo.

Pepper and Natalie went looking for Justin Hammer. He was going to give Pepper some answers. She was determined about that. She hadn't heard what passed between

Hammer and Tony onstage, but clearly things were out of Hammer's control.

"Go away," he said when he saw them. "I can handle this."

"Can you really?" she asked. "Doesn't look like it."

"I can handle this. If your guy hadn't showed up, none of this would have—"

He never got to finish because quicker than Pepper could follow, Natalie had Hammer in an armlock and had slammed him down onto the closest desk. "Who's behind this?" she shouted in his ear. "Who?"

"Ivan," Hammer said when she gave his arm a little extra twist. "Ivan Vanko."

"Where is he?"

"He's at my facility."

Natalie went to find Happy.

Tony led Rhodey and the air force drones on a chase over the Expo grounds. The army, marine, and navy drones marched out through the Tent of Tomorrow's front entrance and started firing at anything they judged to be a target. Tony ducked low and destroyed an army drone, then said, "Let's get this off the Expo grounds."

The marine drones launched into the air, doubling the pursuit. "Rhodey, you still locked on?"

"Yeah," Rhodey said.

"Okay, pull up your socks," Tony said. "This one's about to get wet."

They blasted low over the reflecting pools, kicking up huge rooster tails with the army and marine drones tight on them. He peeled into a high loop, trying to keep the air force drones close and keep their fields of fire angled away from the crowds. He hoped to spring a little surprise when the time was right.

Tony wasn't sure which feature of the Expo was his favorite: the two-hundred-foot-tall steel globe called the Unisphere, reconstructed from the original built for the first Stark Expo, or the reflecting pool. A massive Stark logo stood out above the Unisphere's continents, angling from south to north across its equator.

He flew in a high arc over the lake, War Machine hot on his trail. They'd already seen the reflecting pool, he thought. So why not the Unisphere?

Rhodey broke in. "What's going on up there, man?"

The Unisphere loomed in his sights, and the drones were closing in on his tail again.

But War Machine was closer. Tony ran a targeting projection on the Unisphere, calculating an approach that would get him through it as it rotated without colliding with its longitudinal I beams.

"This might hurt," he said to Rhodey.

"What? No, you are not—"

The way Tony had it figured, War Machine was tight enough on his burners that if Tony got through, so would Rhodey. The Unisphere rotated slowly.

The Mark VI Iron Man suit flew through a gap in the rotating sphere, with War Machine close behind. Tony's calculations were correct: He and Rhodey got through safely. The air force drones, however, didn't.

CHAPTER 34

The Expo was in chaos. Tony thundered overhead, low enough that Pepper felt the wind of his passage. Firing wildly, the air force drones came close behind, with Rhodey an unwilling passenger in their midst. Around Pepper, the world dissolved into explosions. She dropped to her knees. When everything had passed, she looked around again, amazed to still be alive. She'd stayed to make sure Justin Hammer left in handcuffs. Now that was done and she decided she needed to stay until the park was clear. That's what she told the police officers doing crowd control.

But what she really wanted was to call Tony. She'd been trying to coordinate Jarvis's efforts to break Vanko's control over the drones, and Rhodey, but so far nothing had worked.

Coming in low and hot back over the lake, Tony was shocked when he was jerked downward as War Machine caught up with him and wrenched him off course. They both scraped along the side of a building, peeling off a floor's worth of windows and a long line of steel framing.

They shot clear of the building, out toward the edge of the Expo grounds. Tony braked hard, pivoting him and War Machine around their collective center of gravity. War Machine's grip on him loosened, and Tony took the opportunity to fling War Machine—with the unfortunate Rhodey inside, yelling all kinds of things—into the reflecting pool.

But Agent Romanoff was saying something he couldn't hear, and the War Machine armor suddenly went inert. *Uh-oh,* Tony thought. He landed next to Rhodey and heard Romanoff saying, "Reboot complete. You got your best friend back."

"Thank you very much, Agent Romanoff," he said. That was one more thing he hadn't known about her. She was apparently a hacker with serious chops, if she could do that faster than Jarvis.

"Well done with the new chest piece," she added. "I'm reading significantly higher output, and your vitals all look promising."

"Yes, for the moment, I'm not dying. Thank you."

Pepper had apparently been listening in, because her face appeared in Tony's heads-up display practically as soon as he said the word *dying*. "What do you mean, you're not dying? Did you just say you were dying?"

"That you? Uh, no, I'm not. Not anymore."

"What's going on?" she demanded.

"I was going to tell you. I didn't want to alarm you," Tony said.

Her voice started to pitch higher. "You were going to tell me? You really were dying?"

"You didn't let me," Tony protested. "I was gonna make you an omelette and tell you!"

Agent Romanoff broke back in. "Hey, hey, save it for the honeymoon. You got incoming, Tony. Looks like the fight's coming to you."

"Great," Tony said. "Pepper?"

"Are you okay now?"

"I am fine," Tony said. "Don't be mad. I will formally apologize—"

"I am mad."

"—when I'm not fending off a Hammeroid attack," Tony finished.

"Fine," she said in a voice that told him it was definitely not fine.

"We could have been in Venice," he said, remembering their conversation on the plane. That had been the first time he'd meant to tell her about the palladium poisoning.

She rolled her eyes. "Oh, please."

A moment later, War Machine's faceplate flipped up. "Man, you can have your suit back," Rhodey said.

Tony couldn't help but laugh. But they didn't laugh for long. There were more drones to handle, and they were closing in.

CHAPTER 35

They heard a rumble, and blossoms began to shake loose from the trees. The rumble grew louder, its vibrations coming up through the soles of their boots. The remaining drones had arrived. They landed in a precise pattern, creating crossfire but keeping each other out of the planned field of fire. A missile rack opened out of an army drone's shoulders and snapped into position.

Tony opened the comm with Rhodey. "Well," he said. "You ready to make it up to me?"

"I think we got this," Rhodey said. They stood.

Tony didn't waste any time. He stepped up and tore

the rack from the drone's torso. He turned it around as the missile fired, annihilating the robot's upper half and temporarily whiting out Tony's heads-up display.

He let the missile tube drop and said, "That's one."

Rhodey pinned a marine drone down and tore into it with the big machine gun, until Tony finished it off. They were reducing the drone numbers fast, but he wanted the whole thing over with. He powered up a trump card, wrist-mounted cutting lasers that only had a five-second charge.

"Rhodey, get down," he said.

Rhodey dropped and Tony spun in a circle as he fired the lasers. They split all the remaining drones in half, along with most of the trees and a whole lot of flowers.

In the quiet that followed, Natalie—or Natasha—called into Tony and said, "You've got one more drone incoming."

That couldn't be right. They'd been counting.

"This one has a much more powerful repulsor signature," she said.

They looked up and Whiplash came rocketing down out of the sky toward them.

Ivan had been busy designing himself a new armored suit. New whips, too. They deployed from slots at the insides of Vanko's forearms, and could be used as extensions of his arms. They were thicker, longer, and looked even hotter than the ones Tony had seen in Monaco.

"I got this," Rhodey said. He opened up a missile port and fired a minimissile that supposedly could level most bunkers.

It bounced harmlessly off Vanko's armor and fizzled out in the mud. "Hammer tech?" Tony asked. He didn't really need an answer.

Vanko struck at them with the whips. Tony caught one and unbalanced Vanko for a moment, but he threw Tony off and slashed the barrel assembly off Rhodey's Gatling cannon with the other whip.

This was serious. They came at him with everything they had, but every time they knocked him down he got up. Every time he knocked them down, Vanko did more and more damage with the whips.

Ivan roared and went after Tony, who met him full on, exchanging punches for slashes of the whips, which were a lot more powerful than what he'd had in Monaco. Whiplash was doing some serious damage to the Mark VI armor.

Whiplash knocked Tony down and then stomped Rhodey into the ground. Tony pulled him away from Rhodey with one of Whiplash's own whips, but he over-balanced and spun around.

Vanko hit him in the small of the back and hammered him into the pavement. Tony spun, landing a solid elbow to the side of Vanko's head. Ivan flicked a whip that caught Tony's forearm, jerking it painfully backward. Tony rolled with the motion, scissoring Ivan's legs out from under him and stomping on the hand that held the whip. It uncoiled, and sparks shot from the forearm of Vanko's armor.

He got Rhodey around the neck and held him at a distance. Rhodey had to devote all his energy to holding the whip far enough away from his neck so it didn't melt through his armor.

Tony fought, but Vanko got his other whip around Tony's neck. He flipped up his face mask and gloated as he held them both out, waiting for the intense energies of the whips to cut through their armor and finish them.

Tony could feel the heat from the whip through the armor around his neck. The heads-up display was flashing all kinds of red signals. The whips had damaged the suit's control systems. Tony couldn't get up. He couldn't really attack Ivan. And he couldn't hold the whip away from his neck forever.

It was time for last resorts. Letting go of the whip with one hand, Tony said, "Rhodey, I have an idea. Raise your hand."

Rhodey, who was having his own troubles with Vanko's whip around his neck, did. Then he figured out what Tony meant. Could they re-create the explosion that had destroyed most of Tony's house?

"This is your idea?" he shouted. But what else were they going to do?

They fired simultaneously. The two repulsor beams met each other directly in front of Ivan Vanko's face. Their energies intersected and intensified...and then came an explosion that whited out both Tony's and Rhodey's heads-up displays. Vanko's body was blasted backward, and since the whips were still around their necks, Tony and Rhodey went with him.

But by the time they hit the ground, the whips were out...and so was Ivan Vanko. Tony and Rhodey got to their feet and nodded at each other. They'd done it.

But even now, Vanko did not look beaten. He was flat on his back, badly injured, and still smiling.

"You lose," Vanko said, just as he had on the track in Monaco. The RT in his chest turned red and started to blink.

Around them, every other RT in every other drone did the same.

Rhodey figured it out at the same time Tony did. "All these drones are rigged to blow—we gotta get out of here, man."

Good thing the Expo was mostly evacuated, Tony thought. Then he remembered one person who was staying behind.

"Pepper..."

He blazed up and across the Expo grounds, heading for the Tent of Tomorrow. He zeroed in on Pepper, standing on the pavilion steps, with a decommissioned drone not twenty feet from her. There wasn't even time to call, and for all he knew she wouldn't answer, so Tony put himself into overdrive, decelerated hard enough that his vision swam, and snatched her up off the steps just seconds before all thirty-two drones—and Ivan Vanko—exploded in a series of huge fireballs over the devastated Expo.

It was the best fireworks show anyone had ever seen.

When they landed on top of a building a mile or so from the Expo grounds, Pepper took a few steps away from Tony. "Oh my god, I can't take this anymore," she said.

Tony couldn't answer right away because he was trying to get his helmet off. Vanko's whips had damaged the release toggles. "What do you mean? Look at me."

"I can't take the stress. I quit. I'm resigning."

Tony started to argue, but then he understood. It wasn't about the company at all. It was more about him. "You deserve better than me. I understand, let's talk cleanup."

Pepper started to say something else about the transition, and then they both knew what was coming, so they just went ahead and kissed.

"Weird," Tony said when it broke.

Rhodey had apparently landed on the same rooftop without them noticing. "You two looked like two seals fighting over a grape," he cracked. "Listen, I'm going to have to hang on to your suit for a while."

He dropped his faceplate and rocketed away.

Tony and Pepper watched him go.

A few days later, he and Rhodey were in Washington receiving medals. The presenter was none other than Senator Stern, who'd been strong-armed into doing it by Nick Fury. That was Tony's condition for agreeing to join Fury's Avengers thing...whatever that would turn out to be.

As far as Tony could tell, it was some kind of secret organization that kept a handle on people like Ivan Vanko. Maybe others, too.

How many could there be? Tony didn't know. Fury seemed to think he did. Maybe they'd all find out soon enough.

For today, though, it was enough that Tony was in the gang. He hadn't met any of the others except Fury, Coulson, and Romanoff. What did the future hold?

He didn't know. He was just glad he had a future—thanks to his dad—and that it looked like he was going to be sharing it with Pepper.

It wasn't bad being Iron Man.